'I've met men l

'Ah, but have you s
smiling infuriatingl

'What do you think?' challenged Blaize, her
jaw clenched.

'I think, probably not,' he said softly. 'You
lay a very good smokescreen, but really
you're a one-man woman.'

'Well, you're certainly not him,' snapped
Blaize, trying desperately to regain some self-
control.

Cal looked at her disbelievingly. 'No?' he
said lazily.

Dear Reader

Here we are once again at the end of the year. . . looking forward to Christmas and to the delightful surprises the new year holds. During the festivities, though, make sure you let Mills & Boon help you to enjoy a few precious hours of escape. For, with our latest selection of books, you can meet the men of your dreams and travel to far-away places—without leaving the comfort of your own fireside!

Till next month,

The Editor

Sally Carr trained as a journalist and has worked on several national newspapers. She was brought up in the West Indies and her travels have taken her nearly all over the world, including Tibet, Russia and North America. She lives with her husband, two dogs, three goldfish and six hens in an old hunting lodge in Northamptonshire, and has become an expert painter and decorator. She enjoys walking, gardening, and playing the clarinet.

DECEPTIVE DESIRE

BY
SALLY CARR

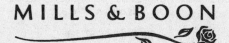

MILLS & BOON LIMITED
ETON HOUSE, 18–24 PARADISE ROAD
RICHMOND, SURREY, TW9 1SR

All the characters in this book have no existence outside the imagination of the Author, and have no relation whatsoever to anyone bearing the same name or names. They are not even distantly inspired by any individual known or unknown to the Author, and all the incidents are pure invention.

MILLS & BOON and the Rose Device are trademarks of the publisher.

First published in Great Britain 1994 by Mills & Boon Limited

© Sally Carr 1994

Australian copyright 1994   Philippine copyright 1994 This edition 1994

ISBN 0 263 78775 3

Set in 10 on 11½ pt Linotron Times 01-9412-54931

Typeset in Great Britain by Centracet, Cambridge Made and printed in Great Britain

CHAPTER ONE

'DAMN, damn, damn!' Blaize thumped the steering-wheel with her gloved hand and stared out at the white world surrounding her car.

Snowflakes were piling up with delicate insistence on the windscreen until the wipers could no longer sweep away their weight. Blaize wound down the window and reached out to push some of the snow away.

The bare white countryside stretched for miles in all directions. She must have taken the wrong turn at that fork in the road about five miles back. Now, from her vantage point on top of a hill, she could see no sign of life anywhere. And the pale December light was fading out of the sky.

What a fool she had been to come out here to the wilds of Oxfordshire in the worst winter in living memory. She should never have let herself be talked into doing this assignment. Living in London, she had forgotten quite how vulnerable a human being could be in the country. Especially when that human being was on the trail of a man like Cal Smith.

Cal. She thought of his photograph in the newspaper cuttings she carried in her bag and swore again. A bit of snow was not going to deter her from getting what she wanted from this man. Especially when she was so close. So tantalisingly close.

She wound up her window and thrust her hands between her legs to warm them up. She couldn't remember being so cold. Not even her childhood had been as cold as this.

Where was that village? It should only be a few miles away, at the very most. She had only to carry on along this road and she was bound to come to a signpost.

It was the thought of the room booked for her in the village pub that was Blaize's undoing. Her foot pressed down on the accelerator and the wheels hit a patch of black ice. She realised she was going too fast to correct the swerve and watched speechlessly as the car ploughed into a bank of snow.

At first, after the impact, it was as though there was absolute silence in the great white world surrounding the car.

Blaize's seatbelt had stopped her from going through the windscreen and, momentarily winded, she took in all the tiny details she had not previously noticed. Like the slow ticking of the engine as it cooled down, the more regular beat of the dashboard clock, and the crunch, crunch, crunch of someone's footsteps coming closer.

'You all right?' The voice was deep, calm and reassuring and Blaize felt a sudden overwhelming relief surging through her veins. She opened her window and focused on two dark eyes, the face shadowed by a jacket hood.

'I'm OK,' she said shakily, not trusting herself to speak further. Truth to tell, she was feeling a little dizzy.

'Good. Let's get you out of here, then, before you freeze to death.' He opened the door and leaned across her to undo her safety belt. Blaize's neck prickled at the close contact, a primeval feeling she had no control over. She was startled at her reaction to a mere stranger and annoyed at her lack of control. Blaize O'Halloran was always one hundred per cent in control of her feelings.

The belt gave way and the stranger drew back a little, still holding her with his eyes. 'You got any warm clothes?'

'I have a suitcase in the back.'

'Keys?'

And to her astonishment she found herself withdrawing the keys from the ignition and holding out the correct one to the boot. The keys to the car! She watched in stupefaction as he took them from her fingers and, with a brief smile, disappeared.

She watched him warily in the rear-view mirror. He could be anybody. A thief. Or worse. The boot lid sprang up and hid him from view. Blaize bit her lip. He was no ordinary man, that was certain. The boot lid slammed shut and his footsteps crunched close once more.

'You sure you've come to the right part of the country?' The stranger's voice held more than a hint of amusement and Blaize's eyes narrowed. She hated to be laughed at.

'What do you mean?' she said sharply.

'From the contents of your suitcase I'd say you were under the impression the Cotswolds were somewhere in the Riviera. There's nothing in there to keep you very warm. Unless, of course, you happen to be exceptionally hot-blooded.' His eyes were mocking, challenging. Blaize compressed her lips.

'What I choose to wear is none of your damn business.'

'It is if you die on me,' he replied coolly. 'We've got a long walk ahead.' Blaize looked at his shadowed face and her heart missed a beat. Just what exactly was this man up to?

'Don't be so damn silly,' she retorted, trying to sound braver than she felt. 'I'm not going anywhere with you.'

'Well, you're certainly not going anywhere without me,' he replied. 'Your car's done for.'

'I only have your word for that,' snapped Blaize. 'And I can manage pretty well by myself, so if you'll kindly give me back my keys I'll be on my way.'

He held out the ring silently, and watched as she fitted the key back into the ignition. She looked up at his still form, outlined in black against the reddening evening sky. 'Haven't you got a home to go to?' she asked tartly, pulling out the choke and turning the key.

Nothing happened. And he was still standing there, watching her. She tried again, conscious of his eyes on the back of her neck. Cold sweat began to trickle down her spine.

But before she could have another go at turning the key, the stranger yanked open the door. 'Get out of the car.'

She stared at him. 'Certainly not.'

The dark brown eyes staring back sparked with annoyance. A strong hand gripped her elbow and half lifted, half pulled her out of her seat.

Blaize found herself standing so close to him that she could feel his body heat. She shook herself free. If she had been six years old she would have stamped her foot. But she was twenty-six, and more rattled by her experience than she cared to admit. 'Go away,' she said as steadily as she could. 'I don't need you.'

'Right at this moment you need me more than

you've probably needed anyone or anything in your whole life,' he said matter-of-factly.

'I doubt it,' she retorted. 'The only thing I need at the moment is to get on with my problems. By myself. I would thank you for helping me but, since you haven't done anything except insult my choice of clothes, I'd be grateful if you disappeared just as quickly as you came.'

She turned back to the car. Maybe this time he would get the message.

'God save me from independent women.'

Blaize spun round. 'What did you say?'

'I said I don't think I've ever met such an obstinate woman in all my life, but I've had just about enough of this tomfoolery.'

His voice grated with impatience as he added, 'I'm cold, I'm hungry and I've got a very good fire all banked up and waiting for me at home. And I'm fed up with watching you make an idiot of yourself.'

'Don't watch me, then,' retorted Blaize. 'I don't need an audience to start a car.'

'You'll never start it,' he said flatly. 'Even if you hadn't flooded the engine with that ridiculous exhibition of female pride, you'd be sitting there until you turned into an icicle waiting for it to move.'

'I can drive, you know,' she flashed.

'I doubt it,' he replied. 'Not when your front axle is broken. Now do yourself a favour and stop arguing.'

'I can manage perfectly well by myself,' said Blaize, pretending a calm practicality she did not feel. 'I'm booked into the Red Lion at Wychwood and I shall walk there myself. It can only be a mile away at the most, down there.' She pointed into the valley at random, hoping desperately she was right.

The stranger's lips flashed into a brief smile. 'The

only accommodation you'll find down there is Ralph Duggen's piggeries and I think you would prefer even my company to his admittedly very fine collection of Gloucester Old Spots.'

Blaize opened her mouth but before she could say anything he reached behind her and pushed the car door shut.

'You may not care about freezing to death,' he said, 'but I do. Now come on. You can call me all the names you're so obviously thinking of while we walk to my house.'

'You could be anyone,' said Blaize, weakening.

'So could you,' he replied simply. 'And if I were a serial killer or a mad rapist you wouldn't be able to escape from me now anyway, so you might as well come with me and hope for the best.'

'I don't trust you,' said Blaize automatically.

His eyes, warm and brown in his shadowed face, smiled into hers. 'I didn't say you could trust me. Even I wouldn't go as far as that.'

Her heart thumped at his mocking tone. 'How far away is it?' she asked faintly.

'A lot closer than the Red Lion,' he replied. Taking the keys, he locked up the car and then turned to look at her. Her wild red hair, the colour of the sunset flooding the hills behind them, spilled like the river of flame down her back.

But her face, normally so mobile, was pinched and white with the cold. Her suit, so smart for a London office, was offering no protection from the freezing temperatures. She began to shiver uncontrollably.

'Haven't you got a coat?' he asked exasperatedly.

'On the back seat with my handbag,' she managed through chattering teeth. He turned back to the car and handed out the bag, but looked in disgust at the short cashmere jacket underneath.

'You call this a coat?'

'What's the matter with it?' said Blaize impatiently. 'It's a very good one.'

'For an over-heated midget,' he countered, his eyes travelling over her tall well-rounded body. 'Which you most definitely are not,' he added.

Blaize watched as he began to strip off his sheepskin jacket. The hood fell back and her jaw dropped as she got her first clear look at the stranger's face. Strong and tanned, with high cheekbones and hair the colour of a ripe chestnut.

It couldn't be him. It just couldn't be. 'I. . .I don't know your name,' she managed at last.

'Pointless giving you my coat,' he said, ignoring her question. 'It's too big and too heavy for you, but this should keep you warm enough.'

He took off his thick jersey and held it out to her. Blaize looked at the strong column of his neck exposed by the open collar of his shirt, the wide shoulders and narrow waist, and then realised she was staring. He glanced at her with amusement as though he could read her mind, and she turned away quickly.

The jersey's rough oiled wool was still warm from his body. Blaize pulled it on and immediately felt better. She watched him put on his coat again.

'OK?' he asked.

'I still don't know your name,' she said softly, almost not daring to breathe for the answer she knew she would eventually get from him.

'So?'

'You're asking me to walk off into the snowy wilds with you,' she said as lightly as she could. 'I'd like to know your name.'

'Smith,' he said abruptly, and then, glancing at her pinched face, his features softened. 'But my friends call me Cal.' He looked at her more closely. 'Mean anything to you?'

'No,' she said as innocently as she could, her heart almost in her mouth. 'Should it?'

Cal Smith. Her instincts had been right. He was much, much more attractive in the flesh than she had bargained for, but it was him. The man she had been tracking for six weeks.

Her fingers tightened around her handbag and her heart quailed at the thought of how he had handed it so casually to her. She didn't want to think about what he'd do if he saw its contents or, more disastrously, discovered who she was.

'Well?' He was looking at her, an eyebrow cocked, a small smile on his lips.

'Well?' she echoed uncertainly, suddenly uncomfortable at the lies she was going to have to tell.

'Don't you think you should tell me your name?' he said softly, too softly for her comfort. 'After all, you're going to walk off into the snowy wilds with me, and I think I should know who you are. For my own protection, naturally.'

The light mockery of her earlier question would have been funny if it didn't put her in such a desperate position. He must not, must not find out her real name. Otherwise he was very likely just to walk her out to the loneliest snowdrift available and leave her there. But if she could fool him into trusting her she was on to the biggst opportunity of her career.

'My name?' she repeated uncertainly. 'Oh,' she said as nonchalantly as she could, while she plucked a new identity from nowhere. 'It's Meg. Meg Bryan.'

'Old-fashioned name,' he commented.

'Old-fashioned girl,' she said and smiled.

He put his hand out and touched her cheek, his fingers lightly brushing her throat. 'I wonder.' Her pulse leapt at his touch and he grinned. 'Well, that's one good thing—your circulation seems to be doing just fine.'

Blaize's eyes snapped. 'Let's make a start, shall we?' She turned her back on him and started walking. After a few strides she realised he was not beside her. She turned to see him standing in the same spot by her car, smiling at her.

'Well?' she demanded. 'Aren't you coming?'

Cal nodded slowly. 'That's the general idea,' he agreed. 'But I happen to live this way.' And, turning on his heel, he walked off in the opposite direction. Blaize swore under her breath, and, sliding and slithering in her thin shoes, she walked, half ran after him.

He waited for her to catch up. 'Think you'll make it?' he asked. She nodded briefly. She would have to.

'Good. It shouldn't take too long.' He grasped her hand as if he had known her all her life and, still shocked by the discovery of his identity, she followed without protest. Once she looked down at the jersey and allowed herself a small smile. On this assignment she really was going to be a wolf in sheep's clothing.

That trip would long remain in Blaize's memory as a waking nightmare. It was pitch-black before they reached Cal's home. But her feet had stopped feeling like blocks of ice long before that—had stopped feeling like anything.

It was as though she had nothing but heaviness on the end of her legs. The cold air seeped through everything, into the very marrow of her soul. It was almost too painful to breathe. The cold seemed to force a narrow band of pain across her lungs.

Her eyelids felt as though they had lead weights attached and soon she was stumbling along with her eyes closed, her hand gripped tightly by Cal. Too tightly, it seemed. Numbly she wanted him to let go so that she could just lie down and sleep in the soft snow.

'Meg?' The voice sounded very far away. Something stirred in her brain. Who was Cal talking to? Her name was Blaize.

'Meg, wake up.' Cal's hand was on her arm, shaking her. 'Meg, can you hear me?' She nodded slowly. 'You mustn't go to sleep. Do you understand?' It was almost too much effort to reply, but she knew she had to make that effort. She nodded speechlessly. He shook her again, more forcefully. 'Answer me, Meg. Say something.'

'Go to hell,' she muttered thickly. Cal laughed out loud and, leaning down, kissed her full on the lips. It was like an electric shock to the system. Her eyes snapped open and a sudden warmth flooded her body.

Cal was kissing her as though he had all the time in the world. Her brain told her to push him away, but her body wouldn't obey. The memory of the way her neck had prickled when he had first undone her seatbelt sparked into life all the emotions she had thought existed only in books. And she knew that she could fall for this man as easily as an apple dropping off a tree.

She wondered if he would be kissing her if he knew who she really was. And then, as he drew her closer, his fingers warm on the nape of her neck, she shut her mind to all the dangerous possibilities and responded with an aching longing in her heart.

At last he lifted his head and looked at her. 'Not bad,' he said lazily, 'for an old-fashioned girl. But then

I've found this sort of treatment never fails to get results.'

Blaize's eyes sparked. 'You arrogant. . .!'

He glanced at her, a glint in his eye belying his mild tone. 'Just thought I'd wake you up. Seems as if I succeeded, don't you think?'

Blaize opened her mouth again, but he grabbed her hand and pulled her along. 'Not far now,' he said encouragingly. 'And then you can tell me exactly what you think of me in front of a roaring log fire.'

'So long as you're on it,' retorted Blaize. 'And I can be poking you with an extra-sharp toasting fork.'

Cal's home was a long, low manor house lying in a small valley. In the summer its stone would look soft and mellow in the sun, but tonight its bulk was thrown into sharp relief by the full moon.

They halted momentarily at the drive gates. 'Not far now,' repeated Cal encouragingly before crunching down the icy gravel.

Blaize paused a moment before plunging after him. She really was on his territory now, and a momentary doubt assailed her. She was deceiving a man who had probably saved her from freezing to death. But then she thought of what she knew about his past and shook her head impatiently. After all that he had done, a few lies on her part were neither here nor there. She could not afford to fail, it was as simple as that. The happiness of too many other people was at stake. But she would have to be careful.

As they got closer to the house Blaize could see its mullioned windows glitter in the pale light and reflect the frosted lawns. Far away an owl hooted and then all was silent again. Blaize thought of graveyards and shivered. She was letting her imagination get the better

of her as usual. Then she started in surprise. Were her
eyes deceiving her, or was there something moving in
the deep black shadow of that old yew tree?

She caught her breath, and then the moonlight
picked out a brindled coat and two glittering eyes. She
pointed speechlessly and tugged Cal's sleeve. 'Look,'
she rasped. 'Oh, God, is there a circus near here? It
must be an escaped lion.' Her heart felt as though it
had stopped. Suddenly it was wonderful to be next to
Cal. She felt for his hand and was immediately
reassured by its dry warm clasp.

He followed the direction of her pointing finger, but
the beast had moved back into deep shadow. Cal
turned back to her and eyed her closely. 'Well, there's
nothing there now. What did you actually see?'

Blaize opened her mouth, but whatever she had
been going to say froze in her throat as she saw the
great beast leave the shadow of the yew and bound
across the snow to them.

She screamed and Cal turned just as it sprang, its
jaws level with his head.

'Conor, you great brute—where the hell have you
been?' Cal plunged his hands into the shaggy fur and
laid his face against the beast's panting jaws, its paws
on his shoulders. 'Get down, you daft old bugger.'

Cal turned to Blaize, his face alight with happiness.
'Some lion, eh?'

'He's more like a small elephant,' said Blaize, stepping out of the way of the furiously wagging tail. 'No
self-respecting dog would grow that size.'

'He's mostly Irish wolfhound,' replied Cal. 'You're
probably related on the female side.'

'You——' gasped Blaize at the insult.

'Save it,' he remarked. 'It's Conor you've got to

thank for my finding you. He'd run off and I was out looking for him when I saw your car.'

He kept tight hold of the dog's collar and fished in the pocket of his coat with his other hand.

'Here, catch.' Blaize caught the keys he threw at her and looked at him questioningly. 'Front door's on a Yale lock; you'll need that brassy-looking key. Open up and make yourself at home while I see to Conor— he sleeps in the stables,' explained Cal.

Blaize looked at the small key in surprise. 'I'd have thought you'd have needed some enormous wrought-iron thing to open the front door to this place.'

'I did, but it was very wearing on the trouser pockets,' replied Cal as he began to walk away.

Blaize, as if in a dream, watched him take the dog around the corner of the house and disappear. Cal Smith had handed her the keys of his house. Wait till the other reporters in the newsroom heard this. No one would believe her, but no one.

She hurried to the door and fitted the key. It turned and the door swung open easily. She stepped inside. No harm in having a quick look round. But how long was he going to be?

Blaize dropped the keys on the hall table and chose a door at random. It opened into a low-beamed sitting-room, complete with the banked-up fire Cal had mentioned. She decided to try another door, but was just pushing it open when she heard a sudden furious barking and some indistinct shouts that sounded like Cal shouting her name.

She walked outside and shut the door carefully behind her. Cal was coming round the side of the house. 'Did you call me just then?' she asked.

He looked at her closely. 'No, Meg. Conor thought

he'd try to chase a rabbit and I was telling him he
could go to blazes if he tried any more tricks on me.'

Blaize's heart thudded at her close escape. The cold
must be congealing her brain. She bit her lip and
stared at her shoes and then looked up to find Cal still
gazing at her.

'Come on,' he said impatiently.

'Come on what?' she echoed uncertainly.

'The keys, woman. Give me the keys. I'm freezing.'

'I left them in the house,' she said slowly, suddenly
realising the enormity of what she had done. 'And I
closed the door to keep the warmth in.'

He stared at her grimly, and then mounted the step
to the front door. He tried the handle, but with no
success. They were locked out.

Blaize closed her eyes and waited for Cal's wrath to
descend on her. She remembered the verbal pastings
she'd had from Barney, her news editor, and shivered
involuntarily. They would be like gentle whispers of
reproof in comparison to what Cal was going to say.

For the first time in her life she, who had always
been calm, efficient, always right and always confident,
felt like wringing her hands in despair. The only thing
that Cal felt like doing, she felt sure, was wringing her
neck.

She opened her eyes and her lips parted in astonishment. Cal was not even looking at her. He was taking
his coat off as if it was the most natural thing to do on
a freezing winter's night. He glanced at her. 'Take that
jersey off,' he ordered.

'What——?'

'Just do it,' he said impatiently, 'or we'll be standing
out here all night.'

Blaize took off the jersey and he put it on. She
shivered in the icy air and he thrust his big heavy coat

into her arms. 'Put it on. I couldn't wear it to climb in, but it'll keep you warm down here while I break in.'

'Down here?' Blaize repeated through her chattering teeth. 'And climb what? Can't you just break a ground-floor window?'

'The're leaded panes,' he replied tersely. 'And the handles are all locked.'

'How very security-conscious of you,' she remarked bitterly.

'I could say the same of you,' he snapped. 'Only it seems that you don't want anyone to get into my house, including me.'

Blaize bit her lip and, for the first time in her life, began to blush. 'I'm sorry,' she muttered. 'I deserved that.'

He stared at her for a long moment. 'Oh, I think you deserve a lot more than that,' he said softly. 'Like a good shake for a start.'

Blaize's eyes narrowed and she felt her temper rising. 'I didn't ask to come here,' she yelled. 'You practically forced me. I'm not any more pleased than you are that I've locked us out, but it's all your fault; you shouldn't have shouted like that. It distracted me.'

'How very thoughtless of me,' he said.

She glared at him. 'And I don't see why you have to go climbing all over the house in the night like a demented acrobat. We could sleep in the stables and call a locksmith tomorrow.'

'What do you suggest we use to contact him—smoke signals?' he retorted. 'Don't tell me, you're planning to do that by setting the barn on fire.'

He stepped closer and looked at her menacingly. 'What's the matter? Suddenly remembered you've forgotten to bring any gelignite?'

'I. . .I. . .' struggled Blaize, but she was no match for his snarling sarcasm.

He looked at her silently for a moment and then, reaching out, took a strand of her hair between his fingers. 'Though I must admit,' he added silkily, 'the idea of curling up with you in the hay does have its appeal.'

Blaize pulled her hair out of his hand, her pulse thundering. 'I'd rather curl up with a mangy alligator!'

'That's what I thought,' Cal replied. 'So, if you don't mind, I'll just climb up my drainpipe and let us in.'

CHAPTER TWO

BLAIZE, her heart in her mouth, watched Cal begin his ascent up the side of the house. The drainpipe was a big old iron one, but it could have easily become rusty and weakened in places, and Cal looked as though he was no mean weight.

She couldn't help admiring the easy way he swung his body higher and higher, using the ivy covering the house to give him an extra hand-hold. He was almost at the top now and soon he would be climbing over the little stone parapet and padding along to the attic window he had told her about.

And then it happened. The last join of the pipe gave way. Cal reached out to grasp some more ivy but it ripped from the wall. For one tantalising second he swung from the pipe and then the brackets holding it gave way and he fell to the ground.

'Oh, my God!' Blaize was by his side almost before she had realised truly what had happened. She knelt over his crumpled form and felt for his pulse. Was it jumping or was that just her shaky fingers? At least he was still alive.

She stood up suddenly and stripped off her coat. She remembered reading somewhere that people who had accidents should always be kept warm. 'Please be all right,' she muttered wildly, laying the sheepskin over him. 'I'll never insult your stupid dog again.'

'Glad to hear it,' Cal mumbled.

Blaize started in astonishment at the totally unexpected sound of his voice. 'You're conscious!' she exclaimed. 'I thought you were half-dead.'

Cal moved to face her and grunted in pain. 'I never do anything by half-measures. What happened?'

Blaize looked at him squarely. 'Your stupid pride made you climb up a drainpipe in the dark and you fell off,' she said brusquely, trying to mask the shock and fear at what had so nearly happened. 'Lucky for you, you hit a flowerbed.'

'I must have some very hard flowers,' gasped Cal. 'It feels as if I've landed on concrete.'

'Can you stand?' asked Blaize.

'I'll give it a go,' he said. 'I think one of my ankles is done for and my right hand is a bit painful.'

Blaize looked at the man she had come to nail for his lies and deceit and could not help admiring his sheer physical courage as he levered himself up off the ground, his face paper-white in the moonlight.

Silently she put on the coat again and bent down to help him. Then, his arm round her shoulder, they slowly straightened up.

'Lucky you're so tall,' remarked Cal.

'Who's lucky?' gasped Blaize as she strove to support his weight. 'Do you think you can make it to the stables?'

The burden eased as Cal put out his left hand and grasped the ivy-covered wall for extra support. 'I can try,' he said grimly.

Slowly they tottered around the corner of the house to the stable block. 'Second door,' Cal muttered, the last of his strength waning. 'It's full of hay in there.'

Blaize undid the bolts and pushed open the door with her shoulder. Conor rumbled a welcome from deep in his chest and slowly raised his bulk to welcome them.

'Is he safe?' asked Blaize, her heart in her mouth at the dog's sheer size.

'As houses,' said Cal, lowering himself to sit on a hay bale. Blaize stared at his foot.

'Considering what you've just done, that's not much of a recommendation.'

The dim bulb hanging from the rafters made the hay shine as Blaize pulled several bales apart to make a good deep bed. The most important thing was to get Cal comfortable.

'I haven't a clue about first-aid,' she admitted, throwing the sheepskin over him as he lay down, 'but I seem to remember something from somewhere about putting accident victims in a recovery position. Aren't you supposed to be curled up on your side with your feet in the air?'

'Physical impossibility at the best of times, I should have thought,' remarked Cal. 'In any case, I'd much rather curl up with you.'

'Hard luck,' said Blaize, her heart hammering ridiculously. 'Let's get your boot off.'

'Well that's a start, at least,' he grinned, his smile slipping slightly as she pulled away the leather.

'It's awfully swollen,' she said doubtfully.

'Bad sprain,' replied Cal. 'I broke it once before, riding, and it's nothing like that. Maybe I've just twisted it. Difficult to tell really, and I'm no medical expert, but it could do with bandaging tightly and an ice-pack.'

'Oh dear,' said Blaize, sarcasm masking the deep relief flooding through her body. 'And my handbag's all out of bandages and ice packs.'

'I'm beginning to wonder what you do keep in that bag of yours,' he said idly. 'It weighs a ton. You must show me one day, when I've an hour or two to spare.

Did you know that what a woman keeps in her
handbag is supposed to reflect the contents of her
brain?'

Blaize stared at him with her mouth open, thinking
in horror of what he would say if he saw her tape
recorder and notebooks. She had completely forgotten
why she was here in the first place. The man she was
just about to spend the night with in a stable was
responsible for the misery of thousands of people. His
whole lifestyle had been paid for with their money.

'What's the matter?' asked Cal. 'You look as if
you've seen a ghost.'

'I did,' she remarked. 'A horrible one.' She shook
her head, as if to rid it of her unwelcome thoughts.
'Now, what about this ice pack?'

'It's like Siberia out there,' Cal said. 'A handful of
snow should do the trick.'

'Bandages?'

A glimmer of a smile passed over his face. 'We
could use your shirt.'

Blaize glared at him. 'I will do no such thing.' She
looked at him lying in the hay. 'We can use yours.'

His eyes, cloudy with pain, stared at her. 'OK.
Whatever you think.'

Startled, she looked at him more closely. She had
expected some more backchat, not this mild agreement. 'Does it hurt really badly?'

He nodded briefly and held out his arm. 'Have a
look at my hand, will you? It might need a clean or
something.'

Blaize found a feed bucket in the corner and washed
it out under the stable tap in the yard. Her hands,
parchment-white from the freezing water, couldn't feel
the snow she scooped from the old stone sundial in the
middle of the U-shaped stable block.

Back in the loose box she set the bucket down and put more bales against the door to keep out the icy draughts.

She looked at Cal's body, sprawled in the hay, and realised it would be almost impossible to get his shirt off. Besides, he needed to be kept warm. She knelt down beside him. 'Promise you won't look?'

'At what?' he said lazily.

'Me,' she replied shortly. 'I'm going to take my shirt off. Promise me.'

'OK,' he replied.

She looked at him sharply and then stood up and turned her back on him. The thin wool jacket slipped from her shoulders, the icy air stinging her skin. Why was she shaking so much? Her fingers fumbled at the buttons of her shirt. She couldn't remember being so clumsy. It must be the cold.

'Let me do it,' said Cal's voice softly behind her.

She whirled around in shock. 'You said you weren't going to look. You promised!'

'I'm a terrible liar,' he drawled, and, reaching out his good hand, pulled her down beside him. His long fingers undid the buttons easily and then parted the silk, pushing it back over her shoulders. 'You have the most beautiful body. Shame to hide it.'

His cool hand caressed her skin, leaving a trail of fire where it went. She gasped, hardly able to breathe, never mind think, as his hand began to undo the catch on her bra.

'No, you can't. You mustn't.'

'Oh, but I can,' he murmured into her hair. 'I'm feeling better already. I must remember to fall off the side of a house more often.'

With an effort, Blaize pulled away. 'You're the most ridiculous man I've ever met. A few minutes ago you were practically fainting with pain and now you're trying to seduce me.'

His brown eyes held hers. 'If it weren't for my hand and bloody stupid ankle, there would be no trying about it, would there? I didn't notice you objecting too much.'

'Stop looking at me like that,' she snapped. 'I can't think straight.'

Cal smiled. 'Thinking straight wasn't really top of my list of this evening's entertainments,' he admitted, and then winced as he moved his foot. Blaize hurriedly pulled off her shirt while his attention was diverted and put her jacket back on.

She looked regretfully at the fine silk and then began to tear it into strips. 'This was my best shirt,' she told him lightly, trying to get back to some atmosphere of normality. 'I hope you appreciate the sacrifice I'm making.'

'I'll buy you a dozen to make up for it,' he grunted as she began to wash his hand. Water droplets dripped off the silk into the hay as she sat and stared at him.

'I don't want you to buy me anything,' she said with sudden venom. 'Keep your money!' adding mentally as she looked at his shocked face, *If you can.*

The hay rustled and crackled under Blaize's body as she tried to get comfortable. It smelt of summer and reminded her of sunlit meadows, but a mere memory wasn't going to keep her very warm in this cold, she thought irritably.

She had lain down a few feet from Cal, as far as she could in the confines of the loose box, but there was no doubt that his presence was disturbing.

And he had been right too, dammit, about what would have happened if he hadn't been injured. He was just too handsome by half. Blaize thought about other men she had been attracted to but none, not even Sean, seemed to have Cal's magnetism.

She couldn't think of one who had made her pulse race in the way he had. And it was probably that very same charm that had made him such an effective crook, she reflected sourly.

'Meg?'

Blaize started. She would never get used to him calling her by that name. Never. 'Yes?'

'Come here a moment.'

Blaize sighed and got up. His foot was probably hurting him again. Thank God she'd never wanted to be a nurse, although Cal was certainly not in the model patient category.

She knelt down and leant over him. 'What's the matter?'

His arm encircled her waist and pulled her to him. 'You are. All that huffing and puffing and acting the insulted virgin. It's keeping me awake.'

Blaize struggled to get up but his arm was like a belt of steel. 'Let me go,' she whispered furiously.

'Certainly not,' he replied. 'A sick man needs his comforts. Well, I'm sick and you're my comfort.'

'Sick in the head, you mean,' snapped Blaize. 'I am not going to sleep with you.'

'Well, you'll just have to stay awake with me, because I'm not letting you go,' he countered. 'Apart from anything else it's much warmer like this, and if you put your head on my shoulder you'll find it far more comfortable than that wisp of hay on those cobblestones over there.'

He pulled her closer so that she was lying along his side, her arm across his chest. 'See,' he said comfortably, arranging the sheepskin coat over both of them.

'Much better. I'd rather have you than a teddy-bear any day.'

'I am not your teddy-bear,' Blaize hissed. But there was no reply. Lifting her head, she could see that he had fallen asleep.

Then the hairs on the back of her neck lifted. Conor had got up to see what all the fuss was about. He licked her ear and, with a contented sigh, lay down on the other side of her.

Blaize snorted. There was no way she was going to spend the night in this position. But she had to admit Cal had been right. It was a lot warmer and Conor seemed to be about as dangerous as a large sofa. She closed her eyes and within seconds was sound asleep.

In the darkness Cal smiled.

Blaize woke with icy sunshine in her eyes and a heavy weight on her chest. She could see the clear sparkling morning through the grimy glass of a small window in the loose box. The weight was Cal's arm.

She raised her head and looked at him. Fast asleep. Gingerly she manoeuvred herself free and laid his arm over Conor's warm back. He muttered something and sighed before lying still once more. Blaize smiled and then tucked the sheepskin coat more securely round him before standing up and brushing off her crumpled suit.

There was hay in her hair and she desperately wanted to brush her teeth. God, it was cold, especially now she had no shirt on underneath her suit. It was amazing how even that thin silk had kept out the draughts. She glanced at Cal, and thought how utterly comfortable he looked, like a panther sleeping off a big dinner. His face was relaxed and totally serene.

Talk about the sleep of the unjust, she thought

sourly. And why did he have to have such beautiful eyelashes? Blaize shrugged as if to rid her mind of such whimsical thoughts and then slipped out of the door.

If it had been chilly in the loose box, it was positively Arctic outside. But at least there was sunshine, watery though it was, instead of moonlight, and Blaize picked her way confidently enough through the crusted snow to the house.

There must be a way into the house, and she meant to find it. Cal's study held the key to his business empire and she was going to lay bare its crooked mysteries, one way or another. She had come too far to back out now.

Her eyes roamed over the back of the house. Locked windows, a solid-looking back door firmly shut. This was indeed the home of a security-conscious man. The house of a man who had something to hide.

Blaize began to walk to the far side of the house and then stopped in amazement. There was a ladder lying against the house wall. An old wooden one admittedly, but it looked perfectly serviceable none the less.

Her eyes sparked as she thought of the night she had just been forced to spend in the stables. Cal must have known about the ladder. What on earth had he been up to, swinging off drainpipes in the dark when he could have used this? He must be crazier than she thought.

She picked it up, the icy wood chilling her fingers, and, panting a little under its weight, set it upright against the house wall.

Little bars of snow were rubbing off on to her jacket and skirt and she thought grimly of how much she had paid for the outfit only a week before. After her adventures of the last twenty-four hours there was no way she could ever wear it again to the office. Perhaps she could put it on expenses, she thought, and then sighed. Unlikely, really, given Barney's legendary penny-pinching. Absorbed in her thoughts of work and clothes—Blaize's driving interests—she began to climb the ladder.

Was it her imagination or were the rungs sagging under her weight? Probably just waterlogged, she told herself, and kept climbing. And then, just as her hand felt for the last rung, there was sharp crack and the wooden bar under her foot gave way with a sickening lurch.

Her heart thudded and, closing her eyes, she gave herself a mental pep-talk as she lifted her foot clear and on to the next rung. She had to go on, she couldn't climb back down now, not when she was so close.

'What the hell do you think you're doing?'

She looked down to see Cal grasping Conor for support, his face grey with worry.

'I'm dancing *Swan Lake* with the Royal Ballet,' she retorted, holding on to the ladder for dear life. 'What does it look as if I'm doing?'

He grabbed the dog's collar more firmly and limped towards her quicker than she would have thought possible for a man with a sprained ankle. 'That ladder's as rotten as hell. Come down before you break your damn neck.'

With a supreme mental and physical effort she reached for the parapet and then got one knee up. 'Don't be silly,' she yelled back. 'Anyway, I'm here now.'

But as she brought up her other foot it knocked the ladder away from the wall. It tottered for a few seconds and then fell, crashing into three pieces on the ground.

For a split-second she swayed dangerously on the

parapet and then swung herself safely over. She crouched on the roof, suddenly appalled at her bravado. Her whole body was shaking at the thought of the risk she had taken.

She stared numbly at her legs. Yesterday they had been encased in flawless ten-denier nylon. Now one knee was bursting through a hole the size of a saucer, and the other had a ladder at last two inches wide.

Blaize put her fingers across the gaping threads and watched the run shoot down her leg. She had been that close to never having to worry about the price of tights again. She shook her head determinedly. This was no way to think. She had to get on.

Gathering her courage, she looked cautiously over the little wall at the scene below. Cal raised his eyes from the wreckage, his face grim. There was no trace of the bantering wit he had plagued her with the night before. Blaize stared back with scared eyes. She desperately wanted him to say something comforting.

But his voice was cold, flat, icier than the water on the stable bucket. 'Open the second skylight along. You'll find it's close to the floor, like a dormer window, so you shouldn't have any difficulty getting in, and then come down and open the front door for me.' That was it. No sarcasm. No words of comfort.

Blaize, who had been dangerously near to tears, felt as though she had been slapped in the face. How dared he speak to her like that?

She swallowed and then scurried away out of sight across a little leaded channel behind the parapet to the window he had mentioned. Who the hell did he think she was? Some brainless little chit? She was a career woman, a hard-nosed reporter with a job to do. As he would soon find out. Blaize stopped in her tracks, the memory of his face in front of her as if he were standing there himself.

She thought, with a sudden flash of horror, of his reaction when he discovered the truth. No. She couldn't possibly tell him who she really was. He would find out soon enough when he read the newspaper about how she had finally proved he had stolen all that pension money from his employees. Perhaps he would read it in gaol with all his crooked directors. And serve him right, too.

She stalked down the stairs like an angry cat and stopped halfway down. There on the hall table was a telephone answering machine, and its light was blinking.

She stood irresolute for a moment and then, her mind made up, ran lightly down the rest of the steps and pressed the playback button. Perhaps she would learn something incriminating about that infuriating man, blast him.

The tape jerked back to the beginning and she suppressed her rising guilt at her snooping. Maybe it would be just a message from the greengrocer. And maybe it would be something that would nail him completely, she told herself firmly.

Blaize bent her head in concentration as the recording began. It was of a woman's voice, low but harshened by obvious desperation.

'Cal? It's Sophie. I need you. Please, please ring me. I. . . Oh——' The message cut off, as if the caller were in a hurry, or had been unexpectedly disturbed. There were no more messages. Blaize's forehead wrinkled. Who was Sophie? Someone involved in the scandal or a girlfriend? Or both?

Blaize found herself trying to picture the woman, and to her amazement felt a hot shaft of jealousy spear right through her. This was ridiculous. She couldn't feel this way over a man who acted so despicably. She simply couldn't afford to.

Angry with herself and her fickle emotions, she suddenly remembered that the object of all this turmoil was even now standing on his own front doorstep waiting for her to let him in. Her eyes narrowing, she straightened her shoulders and marched to the other end of the hall.

She flung open the front door as if answering a challenge. 'Do come in, Mr Smith,' she exclaimed with a flourish. 'Welcome to your ancestral——' but whatever she had been going to add was cut off short as he powered across the threshold towards her, backing her into the wall.

His injured foot seemed to make absolutely no difference to his sheer animal strength. An umbrella stand went spinning and clattering over the floor.

His eyebrows were in one furious line and the sparks in his eyes could have started a forest fire. 'You are the most arrogant, pigheaded, featherbrained female I have ever come across. Do you know what you nearly did back there?'

She felt her temper rising, like an almost physical thing, in her throat. She pushed against his chest but it was like asking Everest to move. 'I don't know about nearly,' she flashed. 'You're the one who fell off the side of a house.'

'I'd like to shake you until your teeth rattle,' he said grimly.

She looked at him haughtily. 'The state you're in at the moment, you couldn't shake a cocktail.'

'Oh, no?' he said softly, in that tone she had begun to realise meant trouble.

'No,' she repeated uncertainly.

His left hand slid under her weight of hair and on down her throat, under the collar of her jacket. The long, sensitive fingers that had so nearly made her forget everything the night before caressed her skin with infinite gentleness.

'You can't do this,' she gasped.

'You're not making a very convincing job of stopping me,' he told her, the jacket buttons coming apart at his touch.

It was true. She found it impossible to protest as he took command of all her senses. Minutes went by, or was it seconds? Her body arched as his hand cupped her right breast, his lips brushing its rose-tipped curve. At this moment there was nothing she would not do for this man. She did not want him ever to stop. She felt beautiful, desired, and utterly wanton.

He drew away from her, his brown eyes studying her creamy body. The jacket was slipping from her shoulders, her skirt all rucked. 'I think you're pretty shaken now, wouldn't you say?' he said.

The delicious feeling stopped as though it had been turned off with a switch. 'You did that on purpose,' she gasped, anger beginning to flash through her veins. 'Like some macho caveman showing who's boss.'

'Partly,' he agreed slowly, reaching out to tuck a strand of hair behind her ear. 'but I must admit I'm feeling pretty shaken myself.'

Blaize pulled her jacket back on furiously. When would she ever learn with this man? He was about as safe as a cobra with toothache. 'Well, hard luck,' she grated. 'I'm not any man's toy.'

'No,' he agreed with a small smile. 'Not any man's. Just mine.'

Blaize clenched her jaw. 'You're the one who could win prizes for arrogance around here,' she said coldly.

'But I'm not surprised you have a caveman attitude to women. You'd have to club any half-decent woman over the head to get her to go with you.'

'I don't recall using a club last night,' Cal said smoothly. 'So what does that make you? Indecent?' His eyes glinted and he added, 'Which reminds me, about that shirt I helped you take off last night. You know, before we slept together——'

'That was different,' snapped Blaize, a slow flush creeping up her neck. God, this man was infuriating. Why did he continually catch her off-balance? And he was standing so close to her. Too close.

'Don't touch me,' she yelled as he reached out a hand. 'I don't need this.'

Cal caressed her face almost as if he couldn't believe it was real. She shivered at his touch. More than anything she wanted to grab his hand, to ask for the comfort she knew only he could give her. But she couldn't. She knew his secrets and she abhorred them.

He looked at the fear in her eyes and sighed. 'Meg, I'm sorry if I upset you. I was so mad with you for taking such a stupid risk on that ladder, I guess I wanted to teach you a lesson. But I think it's rebounded on me somewhat.'

He pulled her towards him and did up her buttons as neatly and impersonally as if he were getting a child ready for school. 'Everything seems to be happening so fast,' he said slowly. 'I've never known anything like it. I feel I've known you all my life. And if my ankle didn't hurt so much I'd carry you upstairs and lock us both in my bedroom until the sky fell in.'

Blaize stared at him, tears spurting into her eyes. This situation was becoming impossible. How much longer could she deceive this man whom her soul desired and her mind rejected?

'What are you so scared of, Meg?' Cal asked gently.

'I'm not scared of anything,' she said loudly and untruthfully. 'It's just that I'm, I'm——' she cast around desperately for something to say, some excuse to break this almost unbearable tension '—I'm married,' she blurted out.

Cal looked at her ringless fingers and raised an eyebrow. 'Really?' he drawled, a suspicion of a smile on his face.

'Yes, really,' she confirmed. 'What's the matter, don't you believe me?'

He was watching her as closely as a hawk with a day-old chick in its sights. 'No, I don't believe you,' he replied. 'What's his name?'

'Oh, er——' Blaize thought of her news editor '—Barney Temple,' she said quickly.

'Your last name is Bryan,' he said softly.

'I didn't believe in taking his name,' replied Blaize, warming to her theme. 'I'm a liberated woman.'

'Really?' he repeated. 'So why did you bother to get married, then?'

Blaize said nothing. Right at this moment she wanted to be anywhere other than here. Beirut would be peaceful in comparison.

Cal turned on his heel and closed the front door. He leant on it, regarding her through half closed eyes. 'Why don't you ring him?' he asked. 'I'm sure you must be dying to tell him you're safe and sound.' He gestured at the telephone. 'Or isn't he the caring sort?'

Blaize glared at him. 'You still don't believe me, do you?'

His eyes glinted back. 'Ring him.'

Desperately she walked towards the telephone. She would have to talk to Barney so that he got the message where she was, without arousing any more of

Cal's suspicions. She looked at his eyes, dark with suspicion, and gulped. That was going to be almost impossible.

Blaize picked up the receiver with a shaking hand and then listened disbelievingly.

'What's the matter?' asked Cal.

She turned to him, trying to keep the relief out of her voice, and said, 'The line's dead. Must be the snow.'

He took the receiver from her and put it to his ear before replacing it on its cradle.

'How very convenient for you,' he said. 'Saves you muttering a pack of lies down the phone at some bemused friend of yours. Although I suppose it also saves me from having to listen to them.'

'How dare you even think about listening to my private telephone calls?' she said hotly. 'Don't you ever believe anything anyone ever tells you?'

'Not usually, no,' replied Cal. He looked at her again, taking in her flushed face and glittering eyes. 'You can't fool me, Meg,' he said quietly. 'You're hiding something from me for some reason, and I mean to find out what it is.'

CHAPTER THREE

BLAIZE pushed her plate away and gazed across the kitchen table at Cal. 'I'm sorry it wasn't very good,' she muttered. 'Cooking is not one of my strong points.'

He chewed thoughtfully and then swallowed. 'What did you say this was again?'

'Egg surprise.'

'Never heard of it,' he said.

'Neither had I,' admitted Blaize. 'Until the first-ever time I attempted to make an omelette, and got this instead.'

He looked at her in surprise. 'And you still make it?'

'It's not that bad,' she said, holding out the remains of her meal to Conor. He got up, sniffed it politely and then lay down again on the flagged floor.

Cal smiled. 'Sorry. He's a bit of a gourmet.'

'So am I,' admitted Blaize regretfully. 'That's why I never do the cooking.'

She waggled her toes luxuriously in a pair of Cal's thick woollen socks. For the first time in ages she was warm. She had had a hot bath and was now wearing one of his old shirts tucked into a pair of outsize jeans. They were held up with an old evening scarf Cal had unearthed from somewhere.

She had insisted on cooking the meal while he had his bath and she had to admit it had been a bit of a disaster. She had never cooked on an Aga before and spent ages waiting for the eggs to cook. Then, when she had lost interest and started browsing through a shelf of recipe books instead, she had forgotten all about the meal until a faintly charred smell had started floating across the old-fashioned low-beamed kitchen.

'Never mind,' said Cal. 'The only thing I can cook is baked beans on toast. Although I must admit I've never really tried doing anything else.'

'Don't you get sick of them?' she asked, surprised.

He laughed. 'I don't generally do the cooking. May does that.'

'Oh.' Why had her heart flopped so sickeningly? It wasn't likely that a man like Cal wouldn't live with a woman. It was just that from all she had read he seemed the definite love 'em and leave 'em type. And where did Sophie fit in? Was she some clinging ex-girlfriend? Still, it would all make good copy.

'What's she like?' Blaize asked, not really wanting to know the answer.

'May?' He looked at her keenly. 'Very beautiful.'

'Oh,' she repeated dully.

'For a sixty-three-year-old.'

'What?' She stared at him in disbelief and he regarded her sardonically. 'May is my housekeeper. She is, as they say, a cook beyond the price of rubies. Which is why I put up with having her useless husband George as a gardener-cum-general-handyman.'

Cal pulled a mug of tea towards him and stirred it thoughtfully. 'It was George who left that rotten ladder lying against the side of the house, the lazy so-and-so. He was supposed to chop it up for firewood before he and May left for their weekend off. You can be sure I'll have something to say to him when he gets back on Monday, and it won't be "Did you have a good weekend?".'

'So it's just you and them living here,' said Blaize tentatively.

'Mostly,' Cal agreed. 'Sometimes I have a friend to stay for a while.'

No doubt female, thought Blaize sourly, adding out loud, 'Don't you ever get lonely? This place is made for children.'

Cal stood up abruptly. 'That's enough questions,' he said. 'You're doing a very fair imitation of the Spanish Inquisition, which frankly, at the moment, I can do without.' Blaize bit her lip. Questioning this man was about as safe as poking a wild animal with a sharp stick. She would have to be much more careful if she was going to succeed on this assignment.

'In any case,' he added with a glint in his eye, 'we have much more pressing things to talk about.'

Blaize's heart lurched. He was going to start asking her about what she was hiding. She kept her eyes on the table. 'Like what?' she said slowly.

He reached out and lifted her chin so that he was staring directly into her eyes. 'Like what we are going to do for the rest of the day.'

She regarded him warily. 'What do you mean?' she said, her heart beginning to thump wildly.

'Really, Meg,' he smiled, 'you have a very filthy mind. Although I can't say an afternoon in bed with you doesn't appeal.'

She pushed his hand away. 'I wasn't thinking any such thing,' she said furiously.

He arched an eyebrow and glanced at her sardonically. 'No? Well, it doesn't really matter because, for once, my mind was on far more dull and practical matters. The barometer is dropping like a stone and with the telephone out of order I can't see us doing anything about rescuing your car. Not that anybody else will be likely to drive along that road in this weather. Which reminds me,' he added smoothly, 'what were you really doing there yesterday evening?'

Blaize stared at her tea for a long moment and then raised her eyes to meet his. 'Talk about the Spanish Inquisition,' she said lightly, trying to head him off.

'What were you doing?' he repeated softly.

'I was going to see a friend,' she snapped. 'Not that it's any of your business.'

'A male friend?' he grated. 'For a cosy weekend at the Red Lion in Wychwood? I'm surprised he hasn't come looking for you. Or will he make do with someone else's company now that you haven't turned up?'

Blaize said nothing. She was not going to tell any more lies than she had to. Let him think what he wanted.

'For a woman with such a touch-me-not attitude, you seem to have a very busy sex life,' he continued. 'Or is that teasing diffidence of yours merely skin-deep?'

'Leave me alone,' she muttered.

He breathed deeply. 'All right, Meg, I'll stop prying. For the moment. But don't expect my patience to last too long. I want to know all about you. And what I want I generally get.'

Cal paused for a moment and then, as if nothing had happened, he changed the subject.

'As far as this afternoon's concerned, we've plenty of food and fuel. So it looks as if we'll just have to sit tight until the weather gets better. It could be very cosy.'

'Like hell,' said Blaize.

'I've heard that's the cosiest place of all,' replied Cal.

* * *

Attempting to cook had not been all she had done while Cal was having his bath. As soon as she had heard sounds of splashing she had slipped outside to the back of the stable block and rung Barney on the portable phone she kept in her handbag.

It was a Saturday, which meant he would be at home. Like all other national news editors, Barney tended to eat, think and drink newspapers, working from early in the morning until late at night when his brainchild was finally produced for the next day's news-stands.

But on Saturdays there was nothing to do. There was no daily paper to be produced for Sunday so he would be at home slouched on his sofa watching his favourite Australian Rules football.

Blaize listened to the phone ring with increasing tension, unable to suppress a sigh of relief when he finally answered.

'You're where?' he barked. She could almost hear him jump off his sofa. She looked nervously around her at the deserted yard and clamped the telephone more tightly to her ear. She had forgotten just how loud his voice was.

'You heard,' she hissed. 'I'm at Cal Smith's house.'

'Actually inside?' said Barney, astonished. 'Well, I'll be damned. The last reporter to ring his front doorbell got chased by some enormous hell-hound.'

Blaize suppressed a smile at the thought of Conor bounding eagerly across the snow to make a new friend. 'If you're talking about Benny Simpson from the *Mail*, I'm not at all surprised,' she said crisply. 'He was obviously mistaken for a rabbit.'

'Well, that's never likely to be your problem,' chuckled Barney. 'How did you manage to do it?'

'Pure fluke, really,' she admitted. 'I crashed the car

on the way to the Red Lion and he found me and brought me to his house. It's so beautiful, Barney, Elizabethan I think—lots of exposed beams and comfy sofas. And with this weather it looks like I'll have to stay another night too.'

'Very cosy,' said Barney, unconsciously echoing Cal.

'Oh, shut up,' whispered Blaize. 'He rescued me from freezing to death, he doesn't have a clue who I am, and I feel like a prize creep.'

'I don't know why you should,' said Barney. 'Even I'd rescue you from a snowdrift and I'm the most unfeeling swine I know. Besides, he's milked millions of pounds from his employees' pension fund and ruined hundreds of people's lives. Just because he's susceptible to a beautiful face doesn't mean to say he's any the less guilty. In my opinion he deserves everything he gets.

'Anyway, look, we've had a tip-off that the police will probably arrest some of his company directors on Monday, but they're being very cagey about our Mr Smith. Personally I think they haven't got enough evidence to nail him. So if you could search his study——'

'But it's going to be almost impossible to do that,' said Blaize desperately. 'I can't simply order him out of his own house so I can have a good nose round. And in this weather I'll just never get the chance. We're together practically all the time.'

'Well, you can't be sleeping with him,' said Barney with searing practicality. 'What about a look-see after he's gone to bed?'

The memory of the previous night flashed across Blaize's mind and she said nothing.

'Blaize? Are you there?'

'Yes,' she replied quickly. 'It's just not as easy as it

seems, that's all. In fact the more I think about this the more impossible I realise it's going to be.' She paused and then asked in a hopeful rush, 'Do you think he really is guilty?'

'As hell,' said Barney. 'Why? You haven't fallen for him, have you?'

'Don't be ridiculous,' she retorted.

'I'm surprised, really,' commented Barney. 'They say he's irresistible to women. Still, I always thought you were choosy.' Blaize said nothing.

'Look,' he added more encouragingly. 'Do what you can. A man like Cal Smith will probably be far too clever to leave anything incriminating lying about, even in his study. But you never know. I'm surprised the police haven't raided his home already.'

'You haven't seen the snow here,' said Blaize. 'It's like Alaska on a bad day.'

'That's true,' conceded Barney. 'Anyway, you've beaten the rest of the pack by miles. All the reporters from the other papers took one look at the snow on the M40 and turned right round again. Not that they have as much on Cal Smith as we do. Just stick with him and see what happens. And if you can get enough stuff to do a piece on his lavish lifestyle, it'll make a really good contrast to one of the people he's ripped off.'

'OK,' said Blaize, suddenly feeling very tired. 'There's just one more thing.'

'What?'

'I told Cal you were my husband.'

'You what?'

'Well,' she said reasonably, 'I can't see him knowing your name. How many ordinary people do you know who would be able to identify the news editor on a national newspaper? It's not as if you ever get your name in the paper. You just spend all your time bullying us and drinking with the editor.'

The silence from Barney was not encouraging. Blaize wondered if she had gone too far, and then added pleadingly, 'Look, it'll take far too long to explain but, if I ring you again and he's listening, my name's Meg Bryan and I'm married to you, Barney Temple.'

'Husband, eh?' She could hear Barney starting to laugh and began to have second thoughts about what she had done. Her lips pressed together. She would never live this down in the newsroom. Not in a million years. Cal Smith had a lot to answer for.

'Well, darling,' said Barney, sugaring his Australian rasp, 'it's very nice to hear from you. I've missed you so much. And if you don't file something about this sneaky so-and-so by tomorrow lunchtime we're heading for a divorce. Got that?'

'Yes, Barney,' she replied meekly, and hung up. She put the phone back in her handbag and walked to the kitchen as if she had lead in her boots.

This quest to nail Cal had started out so promisingly. It had seemed a simple matter of good against evil. But Cal wasn't at all her idea of an evil man.

She knew that if he hadn't rescued her from the snow she would probably have frozen to death. Perhaps she was just letting gratitude cloud her judgement. She sighed. Some gratitude. For the first time in her life she felt sickened at what her job entailed.

Blaize watched Cal drain his mug and then, grasping a walking stick, limp to the kitchen door. Damn her job, she thought with a sudden protective fierceness. And damn Barney.

'What are you doing?' she asked.

'I'm going to split some kindling.'

'But your hand——'

'Much better today,' he said.

She got up from the table and went to his side. 'Show me.'

'It's much better,' he repeated as she grabbed his arm and starting unwinding the thin silk strips.

'Well, it does look as though the grazing's healing up,' she agreed reluctantly. 'But it's hellishly bruised. Can't I help you?'

'Why not?' he replied with a sudden smile. 'You can stand up the wood for me, and I'll chop it one-handed. We don't need very much.'

The sound of the chopping was loud in the winter stillness. The sky was the colour of lead and Blaize hopped from foot to foot with the cold. Cal wasn't looking at her. He was more intent on shovelling the little sticks of kindling they had made into a basket.

She bent down suddenly and, picking up a handful of snow, took aim. It splashed with deadly accuracy over his heart.

Cal looked at the splodge on his coat as if he had never seen a snowball before and then he too scooped up some snow. But he didn't throw it, limping steadily towards her with a curious little smile on his face. More of her snowballs spattered his jacket but he just ignored them.

'Come on, then,' she taunted laughingly, 'throw it. Or is your aim that bad?' Grinning, he reached her and pulled her to him. Her blood was singing with her exertions, her face flushed, her eyes sparkling with more fun than she had had in years.

He was going to kiss her again, as he had done that afternoon, and to hell with the reality of her job. His face came nearer and her lips parted, and then, before she could even draw breath, he had slipped his hand down the collar of her shirt and plastered the snow on her bare warm back.

Her body arched in shock and he kissed her fiercely on the lips. 'That'll teach you to throw snowballs,' he said, his eyes alight with the knowledge of his power over her. 'Now come inside.'

'This is madness,' she breathed. 'This time yesterday I don't think I'd even met you.'

'Maybe it is madness,' he said, his light tone belying the urgency in his eyes, 'but I feel as though I've known you all my life. What happened before yesterday doesn't really count. I want to make love to you, Meg, and I know you feel the same way.'

Blaize looked at his eyes, dark pools in a darkening day, and had a sudden vision of the face of a pensioner she had interviewed, left almost penniless by Cal's crookedness. By Cal.

She pulled away from him suddenly. 'Yesterday does count,' she whispered. 'I'm sorry, Cal. I just can't do this. I can't.'

His eyes hardened. 'Of course, I forgot. You husband. Or is it your lover?'

Blaize stared straight back. 'I have a duty,' she said truthfully. 'A trust. And I can't betray it.'

'Unlike your husband,' said Cal sourly.

'Can't we just be friends, for the moment?' she pleaded. There would come a time when he would never want to speak to her again. And that time was almost upon them. All she really had left with this man was a few hours. A short, sweet time that was doomed to turn into a bitter memory. But she would treasure it, all the same.

Cal looked at her steadily, the hard lines on his face softening slightly at the pain in her face. 'We can be friends, for the moment, yes. But you can't base a friendship on lies, Meg. And you're the biggest liar I've ever met.'

He picked up the basket of kindling and limped back to the house. He stood by the door, waiting for her to open it. 'You know, you remind me of a stray dog I once had.'

'Thank you,' snapped Blaize, her nerves shredding at the emotional strain she was under.

Cal smiled, undaunted at her tone. 'It was a lovely-looking animal but badly treated by its previous owner. Wouldn't come nearer to me than six feet for quite a while.'

'It must have been a very good judge of character,' retorted Blaize.

'She was,' said Cal simply. 'I had her eating out of my hand in two days.'

There was nothing to say to that; the words had not been invented that could slap down his laughing arrogance.

Blaize glared at him, but he had already turned back to the house, seemingly oblivious to her frustrated indignation. She stood there for a moment in the cold, pride making her want to go anywhere but after him, until common sense pushed her unwillingly in his wake. What made his behaviour even more infuriating was that she knew, as surely as if she could see it, that he was grinning all over his damned face.

She followed him into the low-beamed sitting-room and watched as he dumped the basket on the hearth and knelt awkwardly, because of his ankle, to build a fire.

'Why don't you come and sit down?' he said conversationally, his back to her. Blaize felt as though she were glued to the doorway. This was ridiculous. What was she so afraid of?

'Don't mind if I do,' she said in as relaxed a tone as she could muster.

'Here.' He handed her a box of matches, her body jolting as his fingers closed over hers. 'Light the fire. I'll go and get a bottle of wine.' He looked at her closely. 'Do you like wine, Meg?' he said softly.

'It goes to my head,' she said shakily, her heart pounding at the meaning behind his words.

He bent his head and kissed her cheek. 'Good,' he remarked. 'I like it when that self-possessed façade of yours cracks.'

She watched him leave the room, her emotions in turmoil. How could she just keep losing control like this? It was as if whenever he spoke to her she took leave of her senses. She opened the box angrily and said something short and sharp as the matches spilled over the thick hearthrug.

Hurriedly she snatched them up and pushed them back. What on earth was the matter with her? She never behaved like this. She rasped one of the matches over the side of the box and breathed again when it flared into life. She set it to the fire Cal had laid and stared into the quickening flames.

Then, sighing, she got up to close the curtains and switch on the lamps, their soft light turning the room into a haven against the black night. But it was the haven of a dangerous man, something she could not afford to forget.

'Penny for them,' said Cal, coming back into the room, Conor padding after him.

'You'd need a credit card to pay for all the thoughts whizzing through my brain at the moment,' said Blaize with a forced laugh.

'Don't believe in them,' he grunted, uncorking a wine bottle and pouring the ruby liquid into two glasses.

'You're very rich, aren't you?' she remarked, gazing into the depths of her glass.

'Moderately comfortable,' he amended, 'but not very rich, no.'

Blaize thought of the disappearing millions from the pension fund and bit back the sudden retort that sprang to her lips. She was within a hair's breadth of blowing her cover. And she didn't want a row. Not now. Not tonight.

'What about you?' he said, changing the subject. 'I want to know everything about you. What exactly are you, Meg? A princess with a murky past, or just a poor girl made good?'

'You wouldn't believe me if I told you,' said Blaize.

He put down his glass and shrugged. 'Probably not, but with that lovely Irish voice of yours anything you say would be good entertainment value.'

Blaize leant back against Conor's warm bulk and stared up into Cal's dark brooding eyes. There was no reason why she should not tell him some of her background. So long as she was careful. This man was really too dangerous to play games with. She swallowed suddenly, making up her mind. Dammit, she had yearned for years to tell someone. She began jerkily, unsure of how to put it all into words. 'I was born in a racing stable in Ireland.'

Cal smiled. 'I thought you looked at home in the hay.'

'You know perfectly well what I mean,' said Blaize, appalled to find herself smiling back. 'I was born in a house and my father trained racehorses. I could ride almost before I learnt to walk.'

'Sounds idyllic.'

'It was hell,' she said flatly, staring into the flames.

Cal reached out a hand and turned her face to his. 'Tell me.'

'My father wanted a boy. He wanted a son who would be as good a jockey as he had been.' There, it was out, the admission that neither she nor her father had ever really been able to put in exact words to each other.

'Didn't he think of having other children?' asked Cal softly.

Blaize opened her mouth to explain about Ned and then closed it again. In the circumstances it was just too dangerous to mention him. She stared at Cal in sudden confusion, realising he was still waiting for an answer. 'Well?' he prompted.

'I was his first-born,' she said in a rush. 'And my mother died giving birth to me.'

There was silence. Blaize starting stroking Conor's head abstractedly, repeatedly smoothing the rough hairs between his soulful eyes. 'My mother meant more to my father than the sun and moon. He didn't want another wife, and he didn't want me. I just reminded him of her.

'I tried to please him. God, how I tried. I did more work than two of the stable lads put together, but I just didn't have the feeling for horses that he did.

'I mean,' she added, 'if you have an upbringing like mine, riding comes as easily as walking, but my father had that little extra something that made him a great rider and made me just—well, ordinary.'

'I'd like to see you on a horse,' said Cal. 'You have a straight back and a stillness about you sometimes that I bet controls the most difficult horses.'

Blaize looked up at him, unused to honest compliments in general and flustered by getting one from him.

She cleared her throat and looked away. 'Go on,' urged Cal. 'Tell me more.'

'I was good at school,' continued Blaize at last, 'but that didn't really interest him. I ran away, once, when I was eighteen. But I came back after six months. Then just after that, I won a place at university in London, and I came here determined really to show him.'

'And have you?' said Cal.

'I don't know,' she replied. 'I haven't seen him since.' She looked at his probing eyes. Her story was getting far too close to thin ice now. 'That's far too much about me,' she said quickly. 'It's getting boring.'

Cal smiled. 'You must be the only woman in the world who doesn't want to talk about herself. You ought to be in a freak show.'

'And you'd be the one making a profit on the tickets,' she said, adding idly, 'Why don't you tell me about you?'

'Come and sit here, beside me,' Cal replied, patting the cool linen cover of the sofa.

'No,' she remarked with an attempt at a smile. 'It's far too dangerous. I'd rather cuddle up to Conor. I want to know much more about you before I do anything as daring as sitting on a sofa with you.'

'There's nothing much to tell,' he said. 'This place has been in our family, oh, for hundreds of years. But my father sold off a lot of land to pay death duties and then when he died there were more to pay. I ended up working in the City to keep it going.'

'Poor you,' said Blaize, unable to keep the sarcasm from her voice, but desperately following Barney's instructions to get some sort of an interview.

'Not at all,' he replied equably. 'I like working there. I'm a competitive animal and I found I was good at making money. But I still come back here at weekends.'

Blaize looked around at the cheerful comfort of the room. 'It's not very luxurious,' she said, not really thinking of what she was saying.

'Thanks,' he replied mildly.

Blaize reddened. 'No,' she amended hurriedly. 'I just meant that everything in it seems so old.'

His lips twitched. 'Meg, when you're in a hole, stop digging.'

'No, no,' she ploughed on, unable to stop the embarrassment of her tactlessness turning her scarlet, but determined to make her point. 'It's all beautiful, but I'd have thought you'd have a few more mod cons, like central heating.'

'Bad for the paintings,' he remarked. 'Anyway, I find it stifling.' He smiled slowly. 'You could always come over here, if you're feeling chilly.'

'You have all these stables,' said Blaize, pointedly ignoring his invitation, 'and you keep one dog in them. Where are all your horses? I thought you'd have a couple of thoroughbreds at least.'

Cal looked at her and said carefully, 'I kept one hunter, but he was getting on and I sold him last week. I'll be going to the sales soon to see if I can get another.'

All these questions, and all she came up against was blank walls. This was not at all the sort of stuff Barney had demanded. He wanted her to expose a bloated capitalist not a man who, despite his obvious success in the City, seemed to live more simply than she did.

Cal looked at her shrewdly. 'Maybe I should explain, Meg. I like making money, yes. But the money itself isn't important. It's the thrill of the chase, if you like, like a great big poker game.'

'Oh.' Blaize closed her eyes and tried to imprint what he had just said on her memory. It would sound so cruel next to the story of how he had robbed all those pensioners. But she had to get more, much more out of him.

'I thought a City type like you would be more interested in helicopters and yachts than buying just one horse,' she ventured, determined to get something she could use.

'I thought you were City type,' Cal replied. She met his eyes briefly and then glanced away. Why was she getting the feeling that this interview, no matter how subtly she tried to stage it, was going horribly wrong? She felt as though she'd been enticed out on to a sunny beach only to find herself waist-deep in quicksand.

'Helicopters and so on are all very well as toys,' he went on, 'but a yacht's not much use in Oxfordshire.'

'So you do have some trappings, then,' Blaize said, trying to keep her tone as light as possible. There was a deep silence and she looked at him doubtfully to find his eyes once more regarding her as though he could read her brain.

'I notice you stopped telling me your life history at the point where you went to university,' he said idly, changing the subject. 'What happened to you after that?'

'Oh, the usual things,' she replied lamely. 'I got my degree. Got a job. That sort of thing,' she added, stumbling over her words, wondering what she was going to say if he asked her about what sort of job she did.

'Anything else?' said Cal.

'Oh—er, and I got married, of course,' she added brightly. 'I'm really a very ordinary person.'

Cal snorted. 'You really are the most appalling liar, you know.'

She glared at him. 'What I told you about my childhood was perfectly true.'

'Your childhood, yes, probably. But you're not what I'd call ordinary, Meg. And I'd stake my life on you never having married. This blarney about Barney. You insult me by expecting me to believe it. Although you did look suitably guilty about the idea of having a lover.'

His deductions were proving far too shrewd. She had to head him off and fast. 'Don't you dare——' she began hotly.

But Cal leaned forward suddenly, swilling the wine in his glass. 'How many sexual encounters have you had in your life?'

Blaize's eyes sparked. 'That's absolutely——'

'None of my business?' he finished for her. 'Well, I feel it's my business. Everything about you is my business. And I would bet a year's profits on you never having had a long-standing relationship. Maybe just short unsatisfactory ones.'

Blaize stood up so suddenly she spilled some wine on the carpet. 'How dare you say that? How dare you?' she breathed. This man really was the limit!

'I dare because I think it's true,' he replied. 'Sit down. I've got things I want to say to you.'

'Nothing I want to hear,' she said defiantly.

'Oh, you want to hear all right. There isn't a woman in the world who doesn't want to know a man's opinion of her. Especially if it's my opinion.'

Blaize sat.

Cal looked at the wine consideringly and then raised

his eyes to hers. 'In the first place,' he began, 'I know you're lying about a husband because of the way you acted when I met you. There was not one word about this so-called Barney when you discovered you'd broken your front axle. Not one word about having to ring him and tell him where you were. And not one word when I kissed you on the way here. In fact you responded with a hungriness that, for a woman of your looks, surprised me.

'If you really are married you obviously haven't been to bed together for a very long time. But I don't really buy that, so we're back to the possibility of a lover. Is he married? Can't spend much time with you?'

'You, you. . .' struggled Blaize. He'd jumped to all the wrong conclusions about her and there was nothing she could do to make him change his mind. Except tell him the truth and that was not an option.

He smiled sardonically at her. 'What's the matter, lost for words? You're normally so eloquent.'

'I wouldn't dirty my mouth with the words that best describe you,' spat Blaize.

He raised an eyebrow. 'And you wanted to be my friend. Do you have such a high opinion of all your confidantes when you tell them your secrets?'

'You're not my confidante,' yelled Blaize, 'and I wouldn't tell you if you were on fire.'

He reached down and pulled her towards him. 'Which at the moment is just how I feel.'

Blaize opened her mouth to object but his hands were in her hair, her skin thrilling to his touch. Alarm bells were going off in her brain but she ignored them. She would never get tired of him touching her, never.

His lips brushed hers and the wine she had drunk thrummed through her senses. She wanted this man so much she ached. Maybe it wasn't the wine after all, she thought dimly as he kissed her deeply, just his presence intoxicating all her normally crystal-clear reflexes.

Her blood felt like hot honey running and singing through her veins. But as her fingers searched for his face he drew away and looked her in the eyes.

'You want me to make love to you, don't you?'

Blaize blinked and reddened. 'I——'

'Don't you?' he repeated roughly.

'Yes,' she whispered.

He slid his hand underneath her shirt. 'Does your lover make you feel like this?'

'No, I——' she gasped.

But he was not listening, his fingers tracing their hypnotic circles over her heated flesh. 'Or what about your husband?' he murmured. 'Hmm? Does he do this?'

Suddenly he pulled away from her, the contempt and bitterness in his eyes almost too much for her to bear. 'You have the most extraordinary quality of innocence, Meg, but it's just another lie, isn't it?

'All these questions about my wealth and my yachts and helicopters and horses. Tell me, if I really did offer to pay for your thoughts with a credit card, would you make love to me now, here?

'Is that how you got that wonderfully expensive range of finery in your suitcase—on someone else's cheque-book? You said you were an old-fashioned girl, Meg. And you are. And old-fashioned cheap little gold-digger who'd like a bigger bank balance than the one she's got. Is that why you keep pulling away from me? Trying to balance the pros and cons of getting rid of your present source of cash before latching on to me?'

She scrambled away from him, desperately trying to escape the vitriol in his voice. But there was no escape.

'Just a gold-digger,' he repeated. 'I don't know why I didn't see it beforehand.'

Blaize looked at his smouldering expression and opened her mouth to explain. But how could she? She had lied to him. She had set out to snare Cal and had ended up trapping herself.

'It's late,' she said with as much dignity as she could muster.

'Far too late,' he agreed ironically.

'I want to go to bed,' she added.

'I want to throw you out,' he said tiredly, as if he'd proved his point and had no further use for her. 'But I wouldn't put a dog out on a night like this.'

As if on cue Conor rose and shoved his nose into Blaize's hand. 'At least somebody believes in me,' she said unsteadily.

'He has no taste,' snarled Cal.

'Probably why he lives with you,' flashed back Blaize.

Cal's eyes flickered. 'Sometimes I could almost like you,' he said softly, 'if it wasn't that I loathe everything you stand for.'

She stared him straight in the face. It was almost too much to bear to have him saying the same thing about her that she had begun to feel about him.

'Tell me where I can sleep, Cal,' she said as coldly as she could. 'I'll get out of your life just as soon as I can.' She stood up and grasped Conor's collar for support. 'And, as far as you're concerned, that's the absolute truth.'

CHAPTER FOUR

BLAIZE lay rigid in the high feather bed. The house was absolutely silent. Cal had shown her to a room across the hall from his, and she would have delighted in its faded country charm if his manner had not been so cold.

'You remind me of one of those Elizabethan gaolers,' she had told him bitterly as he stood by the thick oak door. 'Perfect manners even when they're sending their prisoner off to the scaffold.'

'You flatter yourself,' he'd said flatly. 'Even Elizabethans knew the difference between a queen and a trollop.'

She had wanted to hit him then. Instead she gripped her right wrist with her other hand and forced a smile. 'Unlike you,' she replied softly. 'But then your dog's a better judge of character than you ever will be.'

Cal's fingers tightened on the big brass doorknob. 'Well, it takes one to know one.' He stared down at her for a few moments and then gestured with his head. 'You bed's over there, Meg. Tonight, for once in your life, you'll be sleeping alone. Why don't you savour the experience? You're not likely to let it happen again.'

Blaize had never really known the extent of her temper before. Had never really wanted to find out. But his words released a boiling rage that almost scared her. No one, not even her father, had been able to hurt her this much.

'You arrogant swine,' she breathed. 'How dare you

say such things to me? You were the one who was all over me last night. You were the one who wouldn't take no for an answer, who backed me up against the wall this morning. And now just because you've jumped to some filthy conclusion about my private life you think you can pass judgement on me.'

She walked a few steps into the room and then turned to face him, her whole body trembling. 'Get out,' she yelled. 'Get out of my life!'

Cal stood and looked at her silently, taking in her white face and glittering eyes. Then he limped across to her and took her in his arms. 'You forget,' he said softly, 'you are the one who has come into my life, my home—even,' he added with a glint, 'one of my beds.'

'Let me go.' She struggled. 'Leave me alone.'

'If you struggle any more,' he whispered, 'I'll fall over and even you wouldn't kick a man when he's down.'

'Just watch me,' she replied fiercely. In answer he bent his head and kissed her. The desire to kick him on the shins stilled suddenly as he took possession of her soft mouth, savouring the sweetness within. Her arms reached instinctively around his neck, her lips parting hungrily under the fierce pressure of his kiss. His hand reached under her jersey and smoothed down the satin bumps of her spine, soothing the jerking tension out of her body until she was as still as a schooled horse.

Every single one of her senses was concentrated on his nearness, the smell of his warm, hard body, the gentle, assured touch of his fingers, the feel of his tongue on her lips. Her whole body was taut with wanting him. But just when she expected him to push her on to the bed he pulled away gently and stroked her cheek. 'It's so easy for you, isn't it, Meg?'

She stared at him in confusion. 'Cal?'

He took a step back and shook his head, as if coming out of a dream. 'Tell me,' he said harshly, 'do you have this effect on the man waiting for you at the Red Lion, or do you only turn it on when you want something?'

Blaize clenched her jaw. The heat was seeping out of her body and she felt coldly sick. 'I told you to leave me alone,' she said thickly, suddenly coming to terms with the fact that he had just been using her to make a point.

'And I should have taken your advice, shouldn't I?' he grated before turning on his heel and limping out of the room. He stopped in the doorway and without turning round said softly, 'Sleep well, Meg.'

'I won't,' she replied bitterly.

She curled up into the foetal position in an attempt to get warmer and heard an owl hoot once in the icy silence outside her bedroom window.

Perhaps it was a good thing it was so cold; there was less chance of her going to sleep. She stared at the bedroom door and the bar of light underneath it that meant Cal was still awake. God rot him.

She pulled the chilly linen sheet angrily over her shoulders and immediately exposed her feet to the icy air of the bedroom. She swore and sat up, reaching for her jersey.

How could the man sneer at central heating? Bad for his paintings indeed. She snorted. A large duvet and a brace of hot water bottles wouldn't come amiss either in this cold. What had he done with all the money he had stolen? 'Probably just gloats over it like some morose dragon,' she muttered to herself.

But that didn't ring true somehow. Cal was the last

person in the world she would have described as
morose. She shrugged, suddenly irritable at her
inability to reconcile the two different personalities
that seemed to make up Cal Smith.

She pulled on the jersey and lay down again, punch-
ing her pillow in a desperate attempt to get some
comfort. It had been warmer sleeping in the stables.
She remembered how she had cuddled up to Cal the
night before and shivered. She might as well have slept
with the devil himself.

Suddenly her heart missed a beat. The light in the
passage had been switched off. She looked at the
luminous dial of her watch and determined to wait for
another half-hour before venturing down to Cal's
study.

The hands of her watch seemed to move as though
they had been embedded in treacle. She kept closing
her eyes and imagining the time had gone, but when
she looked at her watch for confirmation only five
minutes had elapsed. Her stomach tautened with the
tension and she had to keep drawing lungfuls of air. It
was almost as if she had forgotten how to breathe.

Gradually the time went by. She threw the covers
off and sat on the edge of the bed, noticing for the first
time how much it creaked. She did not like to imagine
the scene if Cal decided to investigate any noise she
made. She thought of his probable reaction and shud-
dered. No, such a thing did not bear thinking about at
all.

Her legs came out in goose-bumps as she stumbled
into her icy jeans. Where the hell were her socks? She
felt around on the threadbare carpet for them but
could find only one. She didn't dare put the light on to
see better. Swearing, she pulled the lone sock on and
made for the door.

'Ow!' she whispered furiously as she walked into a chest of drawers. Nursing a scraped knee, she moved to her right and put out a hand. The door had to be here somewhere. Thankfully she felt the cold brass knob under her hand and slowly, so slowly, turned it.

Then, hardly daring to breathe, she opened the door millimetre by millimetre until she could slide through the gap. The big oriel window at the end of the passage was uncurtained. The moon's silver-grey radiance flooded through, softly illuminating a suit of armour and throwing the banisters into sharp relief.

Blaize looked up at the disapproving faces on the portraits of Cal's ancestors lining the walls and, tiptoe-ing with almost exaggerated care, made her way to the head of the stairs.

It would be almost quieter, she thought suddenly, to slide down the banisters. She stifled an almost hysteri-cal giggle as she thought of what Cal's face would look like if he discovered her.

She shook her head impatiently and summoned all her self-control. What was getting into her? This busi-ness was too serious to allow even the tiniest slip-up.

Blaize took each step as if it were covered with red-hot coals. The silence in the house was so complete that even one creak would sound like gunshot.

But she made her way to the study without any sound at all. Offering up a prayer of thanks, she slipped inside the room and closed the door behind her. She leant on the wood, almost exhausted by the tension, and switched on the main light. Blinking in the unaccustomed brightness, she drew a deep breath and made for the filing cabinet.

It was almost too easy, she thought, as she leafed through the files. Barney had been wrong. There was plenty of stuff about Cal's company and it seemed to be couched in fairly plain language. She sat down and began to read.

Her eyebrows drew together in a confused knot as she got to the end of the first page, and stayed that way as she started reading the second. This could not be true. It was simply too outrageous. She stared sightlessly into space. If these papers said what she thought they did, then Cal was completely innocent. In fact, he seemed to have been helping the police to nail his crooked directors.

'What a story,' she breathed, staring at the study door. 'What a brilliant story.' And then her heart flopped like a landed trout as she watched the handle turn and the door open.

Cal was standing in the doorway with an expression that made her wish she were ninety thousand miles away. His voice, when it came, was like a breath from the Arctic. 'What the hell do you think you are doing?' he demanded.

'I'm——' But before she could complete any kind of explanation he had made his way across to her and grabbed the papers from her surprised hand.

He glanced down at them, his expression tightening as he realised what she had been reading. His eyes lifted to hers. But there was no comfort in them. 'Well?' he said. 'I'm waiting.'

Blaize stared at his eyes and felt as though she were gazing down the barrels of a shotgun.

'I. . .I——' she stuttered, not even knowing where to start.

'Oh, I think you can do better than that.' His voice was soft but his eyes offered no comfort at all. 'Come on, Meg. From someone who's so good with words, let's hear it, shall we? What's your story going to be this time? And exactly how much did they pay you?'

'Pay me?' repeated Blaize. 'I don't know what you're talking about.' She looked at Cal's face and was terrified by his expression. There was nothing this man was not capable of and she was alone with him on his territory, marooned by acres of snow. What if he decided to throw her out now, dressed just as she was? She froze to the spot as her imagination took hold.

'I think you know exactly what I'm talking about,' said Cal. 'Now tell me everything you know.'

He reached over the desk and pulled her to him until she was half lying across the broad old-fashioned desk. 'You're hurting me,' she gasped.

He let go of her collar and she narrowly stopped herself from upsetting the inkwell as she flopped over the leather desktop.

'You don't know what the word "hurt" means,' said Cal grimly. 'Your sort just passes around pain the way normal people spread a bad cold.'

Blaize sat up on the desk, rubbing her elbow. 'My sort,' she said wearily. 'You know nothing about me.'

Cal put the files back in their folders and limped to the cabinet. 'I know everything I need to know about you,' he replied, turning round. 'You came here to spy on me. Right?'

Blaize looked back at him steadily. 'Quite right.'

He raised an eyebrow. 'Such honesty. Bit late, though, wouldn't you think, for that?'

Blaize took a deep breath and slid off the desk. 'Your trouble is, you take two and two and make thirty million.'

'That's why I work in the City, sweetheart,' said Cal lightly, only the muscle jumping in his neck betraying his inner tension.

'For God's sake,' she yelled, wanting to shake him out of his complacency, 'I'm a bloody journalist. I came here to spy on you, yes. But only because I thought you were the biggest crook of all time! And now I find you've actually been the driving force behind getting all the real crooks nailed.'

Cal put the folders back in the cabinet and then closed the drawer. He looked at her consideringly. 'They're not nailed yet. How do I know you aren't involved with them, that you aren't just trying to find out exactly what I've got on them?'

Blaize was stunned. It had never occurred to her that he might not believe her, that he could regard her in the same light as she had seen him.

'I'm telling you the truth,' she said coldly.

He lifted his eyebrows. 'Well, that makes a change, I must say.'

'You are the most suspicious man I've ever met.' She raised her eyes in mute appeal to his, but there was no comfort there.

'From the way you've been behaving, are you at all surprised?' he replied.

'Look, Cal, I'm on your side,' said Blaize earnestly. 'I'm not a gold-digger, as you so delicately put it. The only reason I kept banging on about all your money and lifestyle and so on was because I thought you'd siphoned off all those people's pensions, and I couldn't figure out what you'd done with the money. The only person paying me to come here is my editor.'

'Prove it,' he said flatly.

Blaize looked wildly around the room as if for inspiration. The log basket caught her eye and she leapt on it joyfully. A sheaf of newspaper, kept there to light the fire, seemed awfully familiar. She yanked it out and thrust it into Cal's hand. 'Look, that's a story I wrote last week,' jabbing at the headlines with her finger, 'I've even got a picture byline.'

'"By Blaize O'Halloran",' Cal read out icily. 'It sounds just like Meg Bryan.'

Blaize blushed. 'I know. I lied about my name. I thought you might have heard of it. But it is me. You can see it is. Don't go away. I've got something else to show you.'

She ran from the room, bounded up the stairs, grabbed her bag from beside her bed and ran back again. Cal was sitting in the big leather chair behind the desk now, reading the article she had written. 'Look,' she said again, tipping out the contents of her bag on the desktop. At last she could tell the truth. At last there could be complete honesty between them.

Cal's long, sensitive fingers turned over her bright yellow union card and tapped her unsmiling face, forever frozen behind the laminated plastic cover.

He picked up the pink envelope she had taken from the paper's cuttings library, strictly against company rules, and pulled out the thick wad of newsprint. Every single cutting was about him.

He looked at a yellowing photograph of himself ten years before and smoothed out its creases. '"Charles Alexander Lightfoot-Smith, a debs' delight, pictured at the Caledonian Ball last night,"' he read aloud slowly. '"Lightfoot-Smith is known to his friends as Cal on account of his initials, but his growing band of enemies in the City, where he has just made a spectacular killing, no doubt call him something else."'

Cal glanced up at her. 'And you use this as background material? I'm sure it will add a very professional tone to your articles.'

'It's not the only cutting,' said Blaize impatiently. 'I just took everything they'd got.' Cal picked up another, more recent, story. '"Cal Smith, who blazed a trail into the City ten years ago, made another killing

yesterday when he headed the takeover of Benson
Enterprises, the engineering conglomerate. The company had made consistent losses, but has considerable
assets. It is rumoured he will sell off what he can to
recoup his expenditure. Redundancies on a grand scale
are expected."'

'And you didn't disappoint them there, did you?'
said Blaize, unable to resist a dig.

Cal looked at her narrowly. 'People were made
redundant, yes. On very generous terms. And then
after I went to the States and negotiated a very
lucrative deal, most of those workers were taken back.
It was all highly publicised at the time. Or don't you
have the cuttings for that?'

'I may have read something about it,' said Blaize
unwillingly. 'But I was more interested in seeing how
you and your fellow directors had helped yourselves to
Benson's pension funds.'

Cal shovelled the cuttings back into the envelope.
'That is something I am certainly not going to discuss
with you. And if you print one word implicating me in
any fraud whatsoever, I will sue you for everything
you've got, down to your last lipstick.'

His eyes bored into hers and then, glancing down at
the table, he suddenly stilled.

'What's the matter?' she breathed, suddenly feeling
her blood turn to ice.

'This,' he said grimly, reaching for her portable
phone. He pressed a few buttons and then switched it
off again. 'It seems to be in perfect working order.'

'It is,' she said, surprised.

'Didn't it ever occur to you,' he said slowly, as if to
a young child, 'that we could have done with a
telephone last night? The remark you made about
calling a locksmith makes perfect sense now. But it

seems you were quite happy to watch me fall off the side of a house instead.'

'I didn't know you were going to fall,' said Blaize weakly. She looked at Cal's foot and swallowed. 'I bandaged your foot up,' she added desperately. 'You couldn't have done any more with a telephone.'

'My foot wouldn't be like this if you had told me about the phone,' Cal said grimly. 'I could have rung Ralph down in the valley and he could have come across with a spare key. Or, after so graciously letting me sprain my ankle, we could have followed your suggestion and rung a locksmith this morning.'

Blaize felt the blush spread across her face and neck, even across the base of her throat. 'I just forgot all about it. I'm sorry,' she muttered.

'Don't be ridiculous,' snapped Cal. 'You've never been sorry for anything in your whole life. All you wanted out of me was a good story. Even if I'd broken my bloody neck trying to get into the house you would probably have called an ambulance just as a very good excuse to get me out of the way so you could ransack my study.'

Blaize suddenly grabbed the phone from him and threw it across the room. It crashed through the glass door of a bookcase. 'You're the one who's being ridiculous,' she yelled. 'Yes, all right. I wanted a story. And I was prepared to lie a little.'

Cal snorted. 'A little? You've fed me more lies than a Bangkok whore.'

Blaize's eyes sparked. 'How many lies have you told your directors while carefully setting them up for the police, huh?'

'That's different,' retorted Cal.

'Rubbish,' spat Blaize. 'You believed the end justifies the means, and so do I. How far would I have got with you if I'd told you the exact truth? If I'd said to you, "Hello, I'm a journalist for a national newspaper and I've come to find out how big a crook you really are"?'

'The fact remains, Blaize,' said Cal, slightly emphasising her name, 'that you are a journalist and you have been snooping on me. When you get back to your office, what do you think your boss is going to say to you?'

'Why,' said Blaize patiently, 'probably what a great story I've got hold of.'

'Yes,' replied Cal. 'I can just see the headlines now: My Night of Passion with Fraud Scandal Businessman.'

'Don't be ridiculous,' snapped Blaize. 'I don't write stories like that.'

'Don't you?' The voice was mocking now and she felt her mental alarm bells go off. 'Well, we must do something about that, mustn't we?'

'I don't know what you mean,' said Blaize desperately.

Cal pulled her into his lap. 'Don't you?' he repeated. 'Now you're the one who's being ridiculous,' he said softly. 'Ridiculously naïve.'

Her heart thumped at his nearness and sudden change in attitude. He stroked her hair and kissed the blue vein in her neck. 'What an extraordinarily fast pulse you have,' he remarked. The nape of her neck prickled at the heavy sarcasm in his voice.

'Let me go,' struggled Blaize.

'What? And cheat you of a world exclusive? Now where do you think would be the best place?' His fingers were exploring under her jersey, cupping her breasts, stroking her tautening nipples, while his lips kissed her jaw and the soft hollow under her ear.

'What do you mean?' she repeated in a whisper, hardly able to breathe.

She gazed up into his eyes, but they were as hard and unyielding as glass. 'I mean,' he said softly, coldly, his fingers not stopping their exploration of her skin, 'I mean, are you going to take notes now, or do you usually write about this sort of thing from memory? Perhaps you'd like to use your tape-recorder? I must say I've never had my most intimate moments recorded for posterity, but there's always a first time, isn't there? Although you probably can't remember yours, hmm?' His voice was honey-sweet and as corrosive as acid.

'Stop it,' struggled Blaize. His fingers were being infinitely gentle and hypnotic, but she felt as though her soul were on the rack. She would never have dreamt that anything so beautiful could be such torture. 'Why are you doing this to me?' she gasped.

'Because it means absolutely nothing to you, does it?'

'Let me go,' she breathed.

Suddenly his arms holding her relaxed and he sat back. He was breathing deeply as though he had been running hard. Blaize was shocked at the bitter expression on his face.

She sprang from his lap and stood up, crossing her arms across her jersey as if somehow to protect herself from his gaze. 'You know exactly how much that meant to me,' she said slowly. 'But what's really knifing you in the guts is that it means just as much to you and you can't come to terms with it. You're attracted to me but you don't trust me. And you don't want to trust me.'

'And you?' said Cal.

'Me?' replied Blaize. 'I wouldn't trust you if you

came with a twenty-five-year guarantee from Mother Theresa of Calcutta.'

'What a boring prospect,' he drawled, his composure regained. 'And what on earth would a woman like you have in common with such a paragon? The only guarantee you'd get would be one from the gas board—for talking the hind leg off a donkey. But then, being Irish, you must have kissed the Blarney stone. Or was it the Barney stone? I keep forgetting you're married.'

'I'm not married,' screamed Blaize, wanting desperately to throw something large and heavy at his arrogant expression. 'I only told you that because. . .' She stopped suddenly, realising she was on very dangerous ground.

'Because what?' he said, pouncing swiftly on her confusion.

'It doesn't matter,' she muttered. 'You wouldn't understand.'

'Oh, but I think I understand all too well,' Cal replied softly. 'You told me you were married so you could keep your distance. You counted on me backing off if I thought you were another man's woman. But what I'm interested in is why you want me to back off, when you're so obviously attracted to me. Or is it just my bank balance you're attracted to?'

'I don't give a stuff about your money,' said Blaize furiously. 'Or you.'

'Really?' Cal's tone was bland.

'Really,' she emphasised.

Cal sighed. 'You know, Blaize, you're still the worst liar I've ever met.'

CHAPTER FIVE

CAL limped to the bookcase and, thrusting his arm carefully through the smashed glass, retrieved Blaize's mobile phone.

Then he made for the study door, and, holding it open, looked at her impatiently. 'Come on.'

'Come on what?' she said, finding herself obeying his unspoken order and walking towards him.

'It's been a long day,' he said, 'and I'm going back to bed. And unless you want to sit in the dark on your own you'd better come too.'

'Aren't you going to lock the door?' said Blaize, unable to keep the surprise out of her voice.

'Oh, don't worry,' replied Cal. 'I haven't had a sudden rush of trustfulness to the brain. At least not where you're concerned. But since there's not the slightest risk of your being able to tell anyone about what you've read in my private files, I can't see the point in belated security measures.'

'I could ring the office on my phone,' said Blaize. 'In fact, I'm going to.'

'No,' replied Cal flatly.

'What do you mean?' she breathed.

'I mean that that is just what you are not going to do,' said Cal. 'This business is too delicate and too serious for even the smallest slip-up. You can ring your office tomorrow, after I've made certain checks.'

'Even if I believed you were the most honourable journalist in the world, which I don't, I'm not taking

73

the smallest chance on these men being tipped off about anything before the police have a chance to act.'

'You can't do this,' said Blaize. 'I've got to ring Barney.'

'Your husband,' said Cal, his eyes glinting.

'My news editor,' Blaize replied impatiently.

'Such a lot of men in your life,' said Cal with heavy sarcasm. 'And they all seem to be called Barney. How very neat and convenient. But tell me, what do you do if you meet a man with a different name? Demand that he changes it by deed poll?'

'If he's called Cal Smith I just ask him to jump in the nearest lake,' snapped Blaize. 'You really are the limit, do you know that?'

'I love it when you get cross,' said Cal lightly. 'Do you get this angry with your husband and lover?'

Blaize glared at him and then forced herself to draw a deep breath. He was simply not going to wind her up any more. And there was now no longer any reason to lie to him. 'I don't have any men in my life,' she said shortly. 'I have my work and that's it. Any money I have, I earn myself. I've paid my own way since I was nineteen years old.'

His expression changed to one she could not read. 'Don't you rely on anyone, Blaize O'Halloran?'

Her eyes narrowed. Now was not the time to go into details of her private life with Cal Smith. And how dared he stand there looking at her with that expression of pity in his eyes?

'Give me my telephone,' she yelled.

'Sorry,' replied Cal with maddening calm. 'Tomorrow evening maybe, or the day after.' Blaize looked at his powerful bulk and considered rushing him. His ankle would handicap him a great deal.

Cal looked down at her and grinned suddenly.

'Don't even think about forcing it from me, Meg. I could hold you off with one hand tied behind my back.'

'My name's Blaize,' she snapped, reddening in spite of herself. How did he manage to read her mind so effectively?

Blaize crawled back into her bed without bothering to take her clothes off. It was just too cold. The foot she'd had to leave bare felt like a joint left in a supermarket freezer cabinet. She looked at her watch and sighed. Barney would go up the wall if she didn't ring him by tomorrow lunchtime. It was two a.m. and she felt shattered, but not as shattered as she would be when Barney had finished with her.

An outrageous idea struck her. She shook her head impatiently. No, she couldn't possibly do it. She stared at the ceiling and gritted her teeth. She had to. It was the only course of action left open to her. She would wait until Cal was asleep and then creep into his room, steal the phone, ring Barney to put him in the picture, put the phone back and then return to her bedroom as if nothing had happened.

She set the alarm on her watch for four a.m. and curled up once more into a chilly ball.

The beeping of the tiny alarm on her watch startled her out of a clammy nightmare. Goodness, her mouth tasted awful. She swallowed a couple of times and rubbed her eyes. She felt so muzzy. Yawning, she swung her feet to the floor and made for the door. It all seemed like some awful piece of *déjà vu*—the door swinging softly open, the creeping on to the landing. But by now the moon was hanging much lower in the sky and there was only the slightest radiance illuminating the passage.

She felt her way along the wall, and had to stop herself from screaming as her fingers encountered the cold metal arm of the suit of armour.

She clutched it involuntarily for support and then stepped away as carefully as possible; what happened if it crashed to the floor? But it didn't, and she found herself breathing deeply as she reached Cal's door. Thankfully it was ajar. She slipped inside and stood for a moment, irresolute. What if he was awake? She heard Conor grunting dreamily in the corner, and then stepped out tentatively, waiting any moment for the light to blast on and Cal to say something lethally sarcastic. But nothing happened.

She realised she had been holding her breath and let it out slowly. Perhaps everything was going to be all right after all.

Cal was one of those men who never bothered to close his curtains. She could see his body dimly outlined on the bed and next to it a chest. That would be the most likely spot for the phone. She swallowed nervously and kept walking towards it, terrified she would step on a creaking board or trip over his trousers. She could hear his quiet, regular breathing, and took heart. He was obviously deeply asleep.

She tiptoed softly around the bed and made for the chest. The outline of the objects on it was obscure in the dimness. She would have to feel for the phone. Her fingers walked gently around a glass of water, a box of matches, a wallet and then with heart-stopping relief on the familiar buttons of her phone.

As her fingers grasped it, another set of fingers slid round her wrist. 'I'd stop just there, if I were you.'

The bedside light flicked on and Blaize found herself staring horrified into Cal's dark brown eyes. He pulled her towards him and she found herself half sitting, half lying on the bed, his fingers still clamped around her wrist.

'Well, well,' he said lazily, without the least note of surprise in his voice, 'and what an eventful night this is turning out to be.'

'Let me go,' she struggled.

'Uh-uh, princess, not this time.' He looked at her with an ironic smile on his face and then said, 'Let me guess. You just can't resist me any longer so you crept into my room to wake me with a kiss and unleash my simmering passion for you.'

'Don't be so utterly ridiculous,' said Blaize, reddening as she remembered how his caresses had affected her earlier. 'You don't have any passion for me at all, just a sort of curiosity to see how I tick.'

His hands reached beneath her hair and travelled all the way down her body. 'I must admit I don't think much of your seducing kit,' he murmured, ignoring her protests, 'but at least you've taken one of your socks off. Is that supposed to be a sign that I can take off the other one?'

'You know full well why I'm here,' yelled Blaize. 'I need that telephone.'

'And you know bloody well that I'm not going to let you use it,' said Cal shortly. 'And after tonight's little escapade I'm not going to let you out of my sight, either.'

'What do you mean?' Blaize said, a horrible suspicion forming in her mind.

Cal shrugged. 'This bed's more than big enough for two, Blaize. I suggest you lie down here and go to sleep. That is, of course, unless you would prefer to sleep over there with Conor. He's been promoted from the stables, and there's no reason why you shouldn't be, either.' He pointed to the doorway where the great hound had just flopped down, effectively barring any hope of escape.

'Let me go,' snapped Blaize furiously. 'And don't think I wouldn't rather sleep beside Conor; he's got far better manners than you.'

Cal released her wrist and she rubbed it. 'I'm sorry,' he said gently, 'but I can't afford to jeopardise this operation by having you phone your office.'

She thought of the probable consequences of not ringing in to the office on time and swallowed. 'I'll lose my job,' she said starkly.

'Better than losing your life's pension,' he replied. He moved over and pulled her down beside him. She lay as still as a doll as he arranged the covers over her. He rubbed her fingers in his.

'You're so cold,' he muttered.

'I wouldn't worry if I were you,' she replied bitterly. 'I've got a lover and a husband to keep me warm, haven't I?'

'A fictitious husband and a fictitious lover,' he corrected. 'No wonder you're so cold.'

She opened her mouth to say something sharp and crushing, but he laid a gentle finger over her lips. 'Get some sleep,' he said softly.

'I should bite you,' she retorted, pushing his hand away, 'but I'd probably only get blood poisoning.'

He grinned amiably at her and she knew that, however hard she tried to bait him, he would just continue to smile in that infuriating way. It was like kicking Everest.

Cal reached over and put the phone on his side of the bed. 'Now go to sleep,' he repeated, switching out the light. 'Everything will turn out OK.'

Blaize wriggled to the edge of the bed to put the maximum amount of space between them and stared into the darkness. How could everything be OK if she lost her job? It was the most important element of her life. But how could she expect a man like Cal to understand a thing like that? It was obvious from his lifestyle that he had never had to struggle for anything at all.

'Go to sleep, Blaize,' said Cal's calm voice from the other side of the bed.

'Easy for you to say,' she said stormily.

'Not at all,' he replied, 'when all I really want to do is switch the light back on and take your clothes off.'

'Even though I'm nothing but an untrustworthy reporter?' she challenged.

He sighed. 'You're the most irritatingly tempting woman I've ever met, I'll give you that.'

'Thank you very much,' Blaize muttered sarcastically, and then gasped as his fingers reached over and traced her profile.

'The trouble is,' he said gently, 'you're right. I certainly don't trust you and from what I've seen so far there are parts of your character that I don't think I like very much.'

Blaize bit her lip so hard she was surprised she hadn't drawn blood. 'Oh,' she said faintly. It had never actually bothered her before what people thought of her. Now, suddenly, it seemed to matter a great deal.

He withdrew his hand and, propping himself more comfortably on his side, stared at her in the gloom. 'Don't you want to know why?'

Blaize clenched her hands. 'No, because you're such an arrogant big-head you'll probably tell me anyway.'

She scrooged her head under the pillow and swallowed the great sob that was rising in her throat, but he lifted the pillow off and smiled lop-sidedly at her, 'Blaize?'

'Go away,' she muttered. 'I don't know about you, but I've had a bloody awful day and I'm not going to top it all by listening to you list my character defects.'

'We'd still be here until next Christmas if I did that,' he said.

'That's rich, coming from you,' she said fiercely, raising her head. 'Your character defects would fill the *Encyclopaedia Britannica*.' She looked at him and, scrambling to her knees, she counted off on her fingers, 'Arrogance, bloody-mindedness, cold-heartedness, dictatorialness——'

'Is there such a word?' he interrupted.

'Invented specially for you,' she retorted, returning to her list. 'Egomaniac——'

She stopped as his hand closed over hers. 'My turn,' said Cal firmly. He counted slowly off her fingers. 'Feckless, goading, harpy——'

She wrenched her hand away. 'I am not a harpy,' she said, appalled.

Cal rolled on to his back and sighed. 'You're not who you seem, Blaize. Even when you swear you're telling me the truth I know I'm not getting the whole story. And somehow, with you, that matters to me. If it were any other woman lying in bed I wouldn't have any doubts at all about making love to her.'

'Well, any other woman might just lie down and think of England for you,' said Blaize furiously, 'but you're not going to get the chance with me.'

'Thinking of England is the last thing a woman does when I make love to her,' replied Cal lazily.

'That's true,' said Blaize nastily. 'England's too nice. Your lovemaking probably reminds them of Siberia on a rotten day.'

His left hand reached out and pulled her towards him. 'Oh yes?'

'Yes,' she gasped. 'I'm not going to feed your ego, Cal. I'm not going to let you make love to me. You don't even like me. You said so.'

'Maybe I'll just suspend my judgement for this evening,' he said lazily, his hand sliding underneath her jersey.

'No, I——'

His lips stopped her mouth as his fingers caressed her soft breasts. He drew back as his hands stripped away the rough wool, her arms lifting obediently as it pulled over her head. 'God, you're beautiful,' he sighed as he bent to kiss her nipples.

Her fingers entwined in his hair, her senses unable to protest as he deftly pulled off her jeans, and pushed her back on the pillows. 'You don't like me,' she muttered, her lips caressing his warm musky skin.

'No,' he rasped. 'But I want you more than anything in the whole world.' He reached across to the bedside lamp and turned it on. The small pool of yellow light turned Blaize's milky body to soft gold and she looked up into his deep brown eyes.

Every part of her body ached to give in to him. It had been so long, and Cal was everything that she had never expected to find again.

But his arrogance was so infuriating. Downstairs in his study he had treated her alternately like a criminal and a simple child. It was all very well for him to bang on about her morals, she thought furiously. But what about his? It was obvious nobody had ever said no to him.

Their eyes met again and she looked away guiltily. It was also obvious why. Well, she would show him. His hands were travelling up her skin as if he were feeling the finest silk, and she closed her eyes. Even if her treacherous body kept wanting him to make love to her, at least she could ensure he got the minimum enjoyment.

Perhaps if she thought about her next shopping trip. She stared at the ceiling and thought of the relative merits of wool and raw silk.

'Perhaps you'd like a book?' His caresses had stopped abruptly. She flicked her eyes to his. Cal was sitting up, the soft light playing on his well-muscled chest. But there was no soft light in his eyes.

'What?' she asked uncertainly.

'I said,' he replied icily, 'perhaps you'd like a book to pass the time. I do hope I'm not disturbing you.'

He was like a great cat, poised to spring, and Blaize swallowed. This was no game she was playing. And the man in bed with her was no pliant fool. 'I don't know what you mean,' she said hurriedly.

He dropped on his elbows over her, his body covering hers, and she lay suddenly still at his nearness. 'Oh, but I think you do,' he whispered.

'Leave me alone,' she suddenly screamed, out of her depth in his all-consuming presence. Their eyes locked and then she closed hers, unable any more to deal with a situation that was completely beyond her.

She knew without opening her eyes that he had moved away. The sudden lack of his body heat chilled her and she felt a deep despair at the corresponding coldness rapidly seeping through their feelings for each other. When she focused again on the lamplit room he was sitting at the end of the bed watching her.

'What are you so scared of, Blaize?' he said softly.

'I'm not scared of anything,' she retorted.

A long, slow smile curved his lips. 'You're scared of everything, my love, including yourself.'

She sat up indignantly. 'I am not.'

He pulled a blanket round himself and looked at

her. 'You flirt like any normal person and you respond to my advances. But when it comes to making love you lock yourself into a secret world and refuse to come out. Now why is that?'

'Leave me alone,' muttered Blaize.

He reached across and grasped her hand. 'No, I don't think so, sweetheart. That's what you want me to do, isn't it? Just take what I want and get the hell out. Only trouble is, I want what you're not giving.'

She stared at him, a hair's breadth from bursting into tears at his gentle persistence.

'I want you, Blaize,' he said softly, 'and I never give up until I succeed.'

'If you wanted me so much, why didn't you make love to me just then?' she said unsteadily.

'You don't know anything, do you, Blaize O'Halloran? That wouldn't have been making love. That would have been me talking to myself.'

She bit her lip and looked at him. He had come too close, far too close. 'What are you going to do?' she asked stonily. 'Make me feel guilty over something you can't manage?'

A muscle jerked in his cheek and then he smiled and, reaching out, touched her cheek. It was like a jolt of pure electricity.

'Don't touch me!' she yelled.

'Why not?' he said mildly. 'After all, it doesn't affect you.'

She glared at him. 'I hate you.'

'I doubt it,' he muttered. And then, pulling her close, he leant down and kissed her. This time there was none of the gentleness he had shown before. His lips were hard on hers and his hands explored her body with the arrogance of complete mastery. The shock of his embrace left her breathless. 'Well?' he whispered. 'Do you want me to go on?'

Blaize ran her small pink tongue over her bruised lips and nodded mutely. There was nothing she could deny this man, and she had been a fool to try. All of her body wanted him and he knew it.

His fingers were caressing her soft breast, running up and down her milky satin skin, sending a tattoo of desire to her soul. She was drowning in his eyes, his soft brown eyes, and she wanted him more than anything she had ever wanted in her entire life.

She put her fingers to his face, touching his lips, the bump on his nose, fluttering against his eyelids. He reached for her hand and kissed her palm. 'Tell me now, if you don't want this, Blaize, because soon I'm not going to be able to stop myself.'

He tipped her chin up to face him, smoothing away her hair with the back of his hand. 'Well?'

He looked at her motionless face, her eyes cloudy with desire, and then, folding her in his arms, kissed her again and again.

She thought of Sean and the way he had constantly blanked off his feelings from her, and then forgot the past as she stared again into Cal's eyes.

There was no world outside his gaze, a bubble of reality that surrounded them both and excluded everything else.

His skin felt delicious on hers, warm silk with the power of steel, and she knew that no matter what happened afterwards, this moment was a turning point in her life.

He had moved back now, regarding her body as if it were a precious sculpture. 'You're really beautiful, do you know that?' he whispered.

'No,' muttered Blaize, 'I don't,' adding in confusion,

'I mean, I'm not.' She covered herself with her hands, suddenly shockingly aware of her vulnerability, but he grasped her fingers and put them to his lips.

'Never, never hide your body from me,' he said softly.

'But——' struggled Blaize, trying desperately to control her fevered senses.

'No buts,' he replied as he bent to kiss her again. 'Not here. Not now.'

A knot of pulsating desire was loosening irrevocably in her as she responded blindly to him. Her arms slid up his neck, wanting him, needing him. She could deny him nothing. The powerful urgency of his lean, hard body was overwhelming.

She gasped as he moved his body across hers, stroking her breasts, her belly and the softness of her inner thighs. 'Blaize,' he muttered raggedly. 'Blaize.'

And then all words were forgotten as his caresses became more urgent, more demanding. He lifted her body to his and possessed it, and Blaize knew the aching sweetness of wanting him totally and giving completely. 'Cal!' she gasped. 'Cal, please!' She was moving with him now, rhythmically following the path to absolute surrender, willing him to be as one with her as their bodies began to be consumed by the storm that was erupting in them both.

'Cal,' she breathed, the only word that remained to her in this new world she had entered.

'Darling,' he rasped fiercely.

And then she was gone, free floating as the tide broke within her, unconscious of everything save Cal's hard body, still moving within hers before he too was swept away and they were drowning together in the passion they had both created.

* * *

The bright morning sunshine flooded through the window-panes and made diamond patterns on the pale walls. Blaize watched a spider let itself down from one of the old oak beams and then clamber back, like a slow yo-yo. A tear slid out of her eye and she brushed it away with the back of her hand. She couldn't remember ever being so unhappy.

She had let a man who cared nothing for her make love to her. He had said himself that he regarded her simply as a challenge, and she had proved a spectacular pushover. Now he was nowhere in sight and she was probably the furthest thing from his mind.

'Tea, your ladyship.' Cal barged through the door, a mug in his hand. ''Fraid I spilt half of it on the journey up the stairs; my bad ankle kept jerking. But still, it's the thought that counts.'

It was stupid but she could feel her throat constricting as she looked at his face. Maybe he did care a little bit. Bringing that tea upstairs must have cost a lot of effort.

He plonked the mug down by her bed and looked at her. 'What's up? Still trying to plot how to get hold of the telephone?'

Blaize immediately squashed the weak feeling of gratitude over something as silly as a mug of tea. She sat up in bed, holding the sheet to her chin. 'Actually,' she said icily, 'I've got a flock of carrier pigeons under the bed, and if they didn't work I was going to brush up on my semaphore.'

'Very resourceful,' said Cal, sitting on the bed and beginning to sip her tea.

'That's mine,' she said fiercely.

'Workers' privileges,' he replied. 'My, aren't you just bad-tempered in the morning?' He held out the mug and she put her cold fingers gratefully round its warmth.

He watched her drink, and then said, ultra-casually, 'About last night, Blaize.'

She stared at him over the rim of the mug. 'Yes?' she said guardedly.

'I'm not quite certain how to put this.'

Blaize's heart fell through the floor at his deadpan expression. He was going to make some brush-off remark, distance himself from her with some platitude. She could not bear it. Would not bear it. She banged the mug on the bedside table and glared at him. 'Don't try,' she snarled. 'I know it off by heart. You don't like me, but you just couldn't help yourself.'

'On the contrary,' he smiled, 'I did help myself and found the whole process quite as satisfying as you seemed to do.'

She looked at his tousled brown hair and resisted the temptation to reach out and touch it. He didn't like her. All he was interested in was her body. It was as simple and as devastating as that. She glanced at the dregs of her tea and wished it had been laced with a good belt of arsenic.

'I've been reading your diary,' he said, standing up and looking out of the windows over the white rolling sweep of the Cotswolds.

'You've what?' gasped Blaize.

'I found it on the stairs when I went down to make the tea. It must have dropped out of your handbag last night. So I read it,' he said simply. 'I wanted to know about you and I thought you were more likely to tell the truth in that.'

Blaize stared at him open-mouthed. 'And you had the effrontery to call me a snooper,' she said at last. 'At least I had good reason.'

'You flatter yourself,' he replied. 'The only good reason you had was a story for your newspaper and professional kudos for yourself.'

He turned to face her. 'You spent half the night poking about through my private papers, Blaize. It seemed only reasonable for me to have a look at your diary. Besides, when I'm faced with any kind of threat I like to know exactly what I'm facing.'

'Don't be so silly,' said Blaize. 'I was looking at your business papers. That's my diary. It's private.'

He smiled but there was no comfort in it. 'So were the contents of my filing cabinet.'

'It's not the same thing at all,' yelled Blaize.

'Oh, but it is,' replied Cal. 'What's the matter? Don't tell me—you've been fiddling your expenses and this diary contains conclusive proof.' He held up the little olive-green book. She put her hand out for it, but he held it beyond her reach.

Blaize glared at him. 'Give it to me.'

'Who's Ned?' he said quietly.

Blaize blinked rapidly. How dared he do this to her? She'd already given her body to him. Did he think he was going to get her secrets as well, before he moved on to his next challenge? Did last night mean nothing at all?

He smiled grimly at her. 'I'm waiting, Blaize. Although I feel the longer I wait the less likely I'm going to get a shred of truth out of you.'

'Ned is none of your business,' Blaize said at last. 'He's just someone I know.'

'Someone you seem to know very well,' said Cal. 'In fact, so well that six months ago he moved in with you. I've been trying to think of women's names that could be shortened to Ned. But I can't. And I can't imagine you having anything so pedestrian as a male lodger, so I take it he's your lover.'

Blaize's eyes sparked. 'What's it got to do with you?'

He shrugged. 'In normal circumstances, nothing. But these are not normal circumstances, Blaize. I still don't really know who you are.'

'You knew me well enough to make love to me,' managed Blaize through clenched teeth.

Cal sighed. 'Yes, that was very foolish, I suppose, but still very enjoyable, for all that.'

'I'm so glad,' whispered Blaize, her insides turning to water at his cool tone.

He reached out and took her hand. 'Do you regret it?'

She yanked her hand away, desperately trying to look everywhere but at his face. 'Should I? How can I regret something that's meaningless?'

Cal breathed out. 'You really are a four-star liar, aren't you? I can see now that all that stuff about having no one in your life was just a complete lie. Tell me, have you ever told the truth about anything, Blaize?'

'That's rich, coming from you,' she yelled. 'You're the one who said he didn't like me and then proceeded to take my clothes off.'

Cal continued as if she had said nothing, 'Is Ned your lover? Or is he paying you for inside information?' He breathed in deeply and looked at her with studied dislike. 'Although I don't really know why I'm bothering to ask you this when I know I'm not going to get a straight answer.'

'My private life is nothing to do with you,' said Blaize furiously. 'Leave me alone.'

'Who's Ned?' thundered Cal.

'Mind your own business!' she yelled, baited beyond reason.

Cal snorted. 'Now I've heard everything. A journalist who doesn't like invasion of privacy.'

They stared at each other for a long moment. Why did Cal always think the worst of her? She was damned if she was going to answer his questions. Who did he think he was?

To her horror Blaize felt tears welling up in her eyes. She was certainly not going to give Cal the pleasure of seeing those. 'Leave me alone,' she snapped, swallowing the sob that was rising in her throat.

A muscle jumped in Cal's cheek. 'With pleasure.' He threw the diary on the bed and, turning on his heel, he limped out of the room.

'Damn you,' she whispered. 'Damn you to hell fire, Cal Smith.'

But Cal was gone. Conor rose suddenly and shoved his nose under her hand and she hugged his shaggy neck tight. 'Oh, Conor,' she whispered. 'What have I done?'

She had walked into a web of her own making. And now she couldn't get out. Tears rolled down her face as she furiously ripped a sheet from the bed and, wrapping it round her, fled to the bathroom as if all the hounds of hell were on her trail.

She slammed the door behind her and turned on the sink taps to their full extent, splashing her face over and over again, until her sobs began to die.

Her eyes seemed huge in the bathroom's old silvered mirror. 'Like enormous red gooseberries,' Blaize told herself unkindly as she yanked off another six feet of toilet paper to dry her tears.

She sat on the edge of the bath and raked her hands

through her hair. What had she done? she moaned to
herself. What had she done?

Simply slept with the most attractive man she had
ever met, she answered herself. A man who disliked
and despised her, she added numbly. She picked at a
loose thread in the towel. What was the point of telling
him the truth about Ned, when he so obviously didn't
believe a word she said?

Ned. The boy her parents adopted when they were
told they could never have children. Only, as so often
happened, for her to be born a year later.

How she could do right now with his cheerful
presence. They had grown up as brother and sister and
that was the way their relationship had stayed.

Ned would have been a perfect son for her father, if
only he had had any feel at all for horses. But both he
and Blaize had turned out the same with an instinctive
love of books.

Her father had taken it as a personal insult. Which
had been a pity, because Ned had always been so
willing to please. Six feet of amiability. He didn't even
mind when she called him the laughing policeman.
And God knew he had enough reason to resent it. She
thought back to the early years at the stables and how
Ned had always been around to protect her from her
father's screaming rages.

She remembered that awful day when she had come
last at a point-to-point and her father had been icily
cruel in his disappointment. 'Sure, anyone can understand a lump like Ned not being able to ride a seaside
donkey,' he had said, 'but then we adopted him. But
you,' he had said contemptuously, 'you have horses in
your blood.'

'Don't you call Ned a lump,' she had cried, rising to
his defence as she never would to her own.

'I'll call him anything I like. And I'll call him a lump because that's exactly what he is. A sack of potatoes sits better in the saddle than he does. It's my black luck to have just two children and both of them more at home with a book than a bridle.'

Blaize laid her hot head on the cool porcelain of the sink and stifled a sob. She couldn't have told Cal about Ned before. Telling him she had a brother in the fraud squad would have been just too close to home. It had been simpler just to leave him out of the picture altogether. And now, if she told him the truth, he simply wouldn't believe her.

She stood up and stumbled to the door. There was something soft and red lying on the floor, and the tears sprang once more to her eyes as she picked it up. It was her missing sock.

CHAPTER SIX

THE silence between them in the kitchen was so solid it was almost tangible. Blaize hovered over the toaster and mindlessly buttered slice after slice.

'Here, move over.' Cal took the knife from her unresisting hand. 'You're buttering the bread before you've toasted it.'

'Sorry,' muttered Blaize.

Cal laid down the knife and looked at her. 'Why don't you stop pretending, Blaize?'

'I'm not pretending,' she muttered.

'Sure you are,' he said. She looked at his face and saw his expression harden. 'Do you always do this?'

'Do what?' she sniffed.

'Sulk when you don't get your way? My finding that diary must have been quite a jolt for you.'

Blaize said nothing. 'Just tell me if this Ned is anything to do with you being here,' said Cal.

'You wouldn't believe me whatever I said,' she flashed.

He took her jaw between his fingers and turned her face to his. 'You are so right, Blaize. So I'm just going to have to assume the worst, aren't I?'

'Believe what you like,' she breathed, pushing away from him.

'On the contrary,' he said coldly. 'I am the one who has had the wool pulled over my eyes, and I can tell you, Meg, or Blaize, or whatever the hell your name really is, that I don't like it. There are very few people in this world who would play me for a fool, and even

fewer who would then try to repeat the process. Any
who have generally end up begging for cigarette ends
on the London Underground. And that's just the lucky
ones.'

'I suppose the unlucky ones are forced to spend
their entire working day with you,' retorted Blaize.
'No wonder your wife divorced you.'

The silence was so sudden and so menacing Blaize
gasped and put her hand to her mouth. What on earth
had possessed her to say that?

Cal's face was utterly bleak. 'What do you know of
my marriage?' he said softly.

Blaize swallowed. 'I——' She stopped. Her tongue
was suddenly like sandpaper. She had never felt so
unnerved. There was a stillness about Cal that frankly
scared her.

'I'm waiting, Blaize,' he said. 'I want to know all the
nasty little details that you've grubbed up about my
private life.'

'I read about it in those cuttings I showed you,' she
said at last. 'There wasn't very much. Just that you
were married to a former model called Christy Todd
and she left you, and a few years later you divorced on
the grounds of separation.' She looked at him, waiting
for some sort of reaction. But none came. He was still
watching her. It was as if he were trying to read her
mind, scouring it for anything she hadn't told him.

'I don't know why you're so uptight about it,' she
said briskly in an attempt to break the tension. 'Lots
of people get divorced.'

He breathed deeply. 'You really are a vulture, aren't
you?' he said. 'You live by feeding on other people's
lives and heartache.'

'Oh, come off it,' Blaize replied. There was an
overtone in this conversation she couldn't place but it

rattled her. Cal seemed to be going totally over the top about something which was so common these days it was hardly worth mentioning. 'Look,' she said practically, 'divorce is a matter of public record. If I go after someone——' she looked at Cal's face and swallowed '—if I go to interview someone,' she amended, 'I try to find out all I can about them first. It's simply a matter of professionalism. You wouldn't go into negotiations on a multi-million-dollar deal without knowing everything you could about the person on the other side of the table, would you?'

Cal still said nothing.

'Look, what does it matter?' she said impatiently. 'Divorce is no great shame in this country. In fact, it's practically the norm.'

A fleeting memory of that other life she had led once in Ireland rose up before her and she brushed it away quickly. That was then, and this, with Cal staring her into the ground as though he hoped it would swallow her up, this was now. She sketched an attempt at a smile.

'Maybe Christy just didn't like your sense of humour. You and she would probably be miserable if you were still together.'

'Christy is dead.'

The words hung in the air as if they were formed from cold smoke. Blaize bit her lip. 'Oh.' She could think of nothing else to say.

'She died in a terrorist bomb attack in London. I'm surprised it wasn't in your collection of cuttings. Or is it that you just didn't spend enough time on your homework?'

Blaize felt the blood draining out of her face. How crass she had been. How utterly stupid. 'I'm sorry,' she muttered.

'I wouldn't be,' he said expressionlessly. 'She was with her new lover at the time.'

Blaize swallowed. 'I don't suppose you want to talk about it, but——'

'You suppose right,' he replied harshly. 'Pour out the details of my private life to a national newspaper reporter? I see I've done you an injustice; you're even more crass than I imagined.'

Blaize's face flamed. 'I didn't mean an interview. I am a human being, you know. If you'd wanted to talk, I'd listen. You listened to me. It helped.'

'Sorry,' said Cal. 'I'm not in the soul-baring business. And if I were I wouldn't choose a woman who routinely tells other people's secrets to twelve million readers before breakfast. You don't know the difference between truth and fiction, Blaize. You can't even make up your mind what your real name is.'

'You know perfectly well why I told you I had a different name,' said Blaize.

'You change your story so many times over whether you have a husband or a lover, I don't know what to believe any more,' Cal replied wearily. 'And frankly I don't care.'

'You cared last night,' said Blaize desperately.

'Did you?' asked Cal brutally. 'Do you care about anything, Blaize, except yourself?'

'And what about you?' demanded Blaize. 'You were the one who said you didn't like me.'

'How can I like you when I never know whether you're putting on an act or not?' he said. 'The spunky, arrogant woman I rescued from a snowdrift I liked. I admired the way she didn't complain about being dragged miles through snowbound country even though all she had on her feet were a pair of ridiculous red stilettoes.

'The woman who looked after me in the stable, I liked. Even when she nearly broke her neck on that ladder, I admired her bravery. But then I started realising that a lot of what I was seeing was just a front. Just a means to an end.'

'And what about all this pensions business?' said Blaize. 'You must have told a hell of a lot of lies to your fellow directors while carefully luring them into a trap.'

'That's different,' snapped Cal.

'No, it's not, and you know it. Some of them could be perfectly innocent.'

Black smoke began to billow from the toaster. 'Don't dig in it with your knife,' yelled Cal. 'You'll fuse the wretched thing.'

Blaize glared at him, unplugged it and, yanking open the door, threw the whole thing outside. It landed with a thump in a flurry of snow. The blackened squares of toast somersaulted out of it, Conor joyfully chasing them.

She called him in crossly and slammed the door so hard the glass rattled. Cal stared at her stonily. 'You lied to me because you wanted a story,' he accused. 'You wanted to expose me for being some sort of crook. I lied to those men because shortly after I took over the company I realised how many people's futures they were trying to wreck. You care only about yourself, Blaize. I lied because I was trying to do the best I could for a lot of people who trusted me.'

'Your trouble is, you think you have a monopoly on honour,' she retorted.

'And you don't have any at all,' he said softly.

'That's monstrous,' she replied sharply.

'Is it?' he said. 'We both know if I wanted to make

love to you now, here, you wouldn't object. Would you?'

He grabbed her hands and pulled her towards him. 'Would you? And what would it mean to you? I'll tell you: just what I now realise it meant to you last night. Absolutely nothing. Even when you make love,' he added contemptuously, 'you just can't stop lying.'

They stared at each other, the air between them heavy with misunderstanding. But they were startled out of their silence by the telephone ringing. 'It's working again,' said Blaize unnecessarily.

'So it would seem,' agreed Cal grimly, dropping her hands and limping to the hall.

Blaize flopped into one of the kitchen chairs and looked at the slice of toast on her plate. She couldn't face even the thought of food. She spread it with strawberry jam and, holding it out to an astonished Conor, scratched his head while his jaws engulfed it.

'That was the police,' said Cal, returning. 'The arrests all went off without a hitch this morning.'

'But they were supposed to happen tomorrow,' said Blaize in surprise.

'How did you know that?' said Cal.

Blaize thought of her illicit phone call to Barney and lowered her gaze. 'I just did.'

He stared at her for a few seconds. 'Yes, well, apparently that's what they all believed too. It seems they'd just been tipped off when the police arrived. One of them was getting in a car for the airport when he was arrested. I wonder who told them?'

'Not me,' she said flatly. 'Someone took my telephone from me, remember?'

'You should be glad I've given you such a cast-iron alibi,' he said softly, 'because if I can prove you are acting as a paid informer instead of a blundering journalist your life will not be worth living.'

He sighed and then added, 'There's a police car on the way to pick me up, because they need me in London to help them with the final details of the case. You'd better come along too. I shouldn't think there'll be any problem about you getting a lift back with me.'

'Do I have any choice in the matter?' demanded Blaize.

'No,' he replied simply.

'And suppose I say no?' she asked.

'Don't even suppose it,' retorted Cal. 'I've still got one or two question marks against your name. Any sort of refusal is just going to strengthen them. In any case, I expect the police will want to question you.'

'I doubt it,' said Blaize. 'My relationship with the police is pretty close.'

Cal raised an eyebrow. 'Don't tell me—you've slept with the whole of Scotland Yard.'

Blaize glared at him. 'That was a pretty cheap crack, even for you.'

He shrugged his shoulders wearily. 'I apologise.'

There was something in his tone that filled her with sadness for what might have been. 'So do I,' she muttered.

They stared at each other for a long moment. Blaize wanted nothing more than to hurl herself into his arms. But the only comfort she would get from Cal would be superficial, physical and, to him, meaningless. It was like a knife in her heart.

She swallowed and stared woodenly at him, forcing herself to speak calmly. 'I'm going to ring the AA about my car, and then my office, if that's all right with you, of course.'

He nodded slowly as if he hadn't really heard her. 'Fine.'

Blaize thought of the exclusive world their passion had built the night before. Now, suddenly, they could almost have been strangers exchanging the time of day on a railway station platform.

She got up and made her way blindly from the room. Her abandoned car was an easy problem to fix. Barney proved not so tractable. 'What a brilliant story,' he enthused. 'Brilliant,' he repeated.

'Shame we can't use any of it,' said Blaize. 'Now that the men have been charged, all these details can't be published until after the trial.'

'Yes, but think of the exclusive interview we can run with Cal Smith,' said Barney. '"My Weekend with Snowbound Pensions Scandal Boss"—I can just see it now.'

Blaize shivered. It was all horribly as Cal had foreseen. 'I'm afraid I can't do that,' she said slowly.

'What?' demanded Barney. 'What on earth are you on about, "can't do it"? And don't tell me it's because of this stupid rumour going around.'

'What rumour?' said Blaize, momentarily pushed off balance.

'The rumour about your Mr Smith,' said Barney with maddening slowness.

'He's not my Mr Smith,' said Blaize crisply. 'Stop playing games, Barney. What's going on?'

'Nothing much,' her boss replied. 'Just that over the weekend the grapevine's begun to hum with speculation that your Mr—' Barney stopped. Blaize remained silent. She would wring this story out of him if she had to hang on to the telephone all day. Blast him.

'Sorry, Blaize,' amended Barney. 'I just so like

winding you up. The rumour is that Cal Smith is negotiating to buy *The Morning News*.'

'What?' gasped Blaize. 'You are joking.' The idea of Cal owning her newspaper, interfering in everything she held so dear, was like a bucket of icy water in the face.

'I'm not joking, but it is just a rumour,' said Barney. 'I asked the editor about it but he either knows nothing or he's just not telling. The latter, I suspect. Anyway, until we get anything more concrete about him buying us up I want you to go ahead as normal. Now what about this profile?'

'The answer's still no, Barney. I didn't become a journalist to write sleazy details of people's private lives,' retorted Blaize.

'Well, you've certainly never had any qualms about it before,' countered Barney. 'What's the matter? Finally fallen for him?'

'You can say what you like, Barney. I'm not doing it.'

'Then you're fired.'

'Barney?' But there was just a monotone whine to show that her boss, her now erstwhile boss it seemed, had hung up.

She dragged herself upstairs and changed out of the jeans and jumper Cal had lent her. Her suit was definitely not the delight to the eye it had been forty-eight hours ago. Her tights had more ladders in them than a DIY store and her shoes, her precious red stilettoes, were irreparably scuffed.

Not that it mattered what she looked like any more. She didn't have a job and Cal hated her. She glared at herself in the mirror. 'Stop being so pathetic,' she told her reflection. What was a job when so many people had a much worse life than she did?

The crunch of gravel outside broke into her intro-spection. A car had arrived, probably the police for Cal.

She went to the head of the stairs as the doorbell rang, and watched Cal answer it. There on the door-step was a tall young man with hair that wouldn't lie flat no matter what he did to it, and a mouth that looked as though it was always just waiting for the chance to smile. She must be dreaming. The officer sent to collect Cal was Ned.

'Afternoon, sir, all ready?' Ned's eyes moved past Cal and widened in surprise as he saw Blaize. But before she could say anything she had flung herself downstairs and into his arms.

At last a friendly face. And it belonged to someone she could trust absolutely. 'Ned! How wonderful to see you again!'

'Blaize!' Ned, infected by her joy, swung her up in his arms. 'What on earth are you doing here?'

'Work,' she said grimly. And then she caught sight of Cal's face. His black expression made her heart miss a beat for one second, and then the idea for revenge took over. She looked at him sweetly and, tucking her arm through Ned's, said, 'I don't know if you two have already been introduced but, Cal, this is my fiancé, Ned.'

She pressed her fingers urgently on Ned's arm, willing him not to blurt out the truth. Cal's eyes narrowed and he looked on the verge of saying some-thing really crushing. A second passed. Or was it two? Blaize stared him straight in the eyes. 'Now do you believe I'm on the straight and level?'

Cal stared coldly back at Blaize. 'Ned and I know each other already,' he told her, 'but not terribly well, it seems.'

He turned abruptly to his study. 'I have to get some papers. I'll be five minutes.'

Ned watched his departing back with some amazement and then turnd to Blaize. 'Wow, sis, what on earth is going on? Cal looked like he wanted to kill me with his bare hands.'

'Not you,' corrected Blaize. 'Me. And the feeling's mutual.'

Ned looked at her wonderingly. 'What's happened here this weekend, Blaize? I've never seen you look so washed out.'

'Oh, nothing much,' she said, forcing a lightness she didn't feel into her words. 'I've just locked him out of his house in the middle of the night, which led to him falling off a drainpipe and spraining his ankle. I also rifled through his private papers, accused him of massive fraud and——'

'There's an "and" to all that?' said Ned in astonishment.

Blaize opened her mouth and then closed it again. The study door was opening. 'I'll tell you later,' she whispered quickly. 'I'm sorry about this fiancé business, but please back me up.'

Ned shrugged his agreement. Blaize was normally so straight and open. But something was making her act very strangely indeed. And you didn't need to be Sherlock Holmes to figure where the blame lay. What had Cal Smith been up to now?

As Cal emerged from the study Blaize surrendered to her overwhelming desire to kick him where it hurt, right in the middle of his damn male pride. Throwing her arms round Ned, she said, 'Oh, I do love you, Ned. You're so wonderful.'

'Natural gift,' replied Ned, grinning rather sheepishly. He looked at Cal's impassive face and hurriedly disentangled Blaize's arms. 'All ready, sir?'

Cal turned to Blaize and stared at her as if she were some servant he distantly remembered. 'Do you think you could manage to spare some time to put Conor in the stable and make sure he has sufficient fresh water? May and George will be back later tonight so he won't be on his own for very long.'

It was the last thing she had expected him to say. She had been so ready to slap down any smart remark that he cared to come out with that she was completely floored by his concern for his dog.

'Of course,' she said weakly. She made for the kitchen, knowing that both men's eyes were on her back, and took Conor by the collar. She bit her lip as she opened the back door. Why couldn't she have looked Cal in the eye when he spoke to her? The man was a complete rat. So why was she the one who felt at such a disadvantage?

She gave Conor one last hug and locked him in the loose box. Strange to think of how she had been so terrified of him when she had first seen him, and now it was a real wrench to think she would probably never see him again. Nor, after today, his master.

She squashed down the sudden feeling of loneliness at the idea of not having Cal in her life. Why should she be feeling such a ridiculous emotion? He didn't care for her and she didn't care for him.

But her depression must have shown when she walked round to the front of the house, because Ned instinctively reached for her hand and squeezed it. 'Cheer up, Blaize, we'll soon be home.'

All of which did nothing to better Cal's temper. He sat in absolute silence in the front of the police Range Rover until Ned pulled off the motorway for petrol.

Blaize sat and stared at the back of Cal's head,
willing him to turn round, but to no avail. 'I think I'll
just go and get some chocolate,' she said quickly,
reaching for the door-handle.

'Tell me,' said Cal, still staring through the windscreen, 'are you really going to get some chocolate or
do you just want to compare scripts with Ned?'

'I don't know what you mean,' Blaize said uneasily.

Cal turned to her. There was a glint in his eye that
made her feel distinctly uncomfortable. 'Funny thing,
Blaize. After this weekend I would have sworn that
you would always know exactly what I mean.'

She dropped her eyes.

'Why don't you tell me the truth and stop this silly
charade?' he said.

Blaize clenched her jaw. 'Don't patronise me,' she
replied icily.

'Patronise you?' he drawled. 'That's what people do
to restaurants, isn't it?' He was making fun of her
again. Goddamn him. Oh, how she hated that.

Her lips twisted angrily. Why should she give him
the pleasure of admitting she was lying to him? She
looked out of the window and snorted. Arrogant
know-all.

'Go to hell,' she snarled.

There was silence and then Cal turned more fully
round in his seat to look at her. 'OK, Blaize,' he
sighed. 'Let's play it your way. Let's assume you and
Ned are romantically involved.'

Blaize stared at him, saying nothing.

'Shall we assume that?' he said gently.

She shrugged, not trusting herself to speak. What
was he up to now?

'OK,' he resumed. 'In that case, does he know how
much you give him the runaround?'

'I do not give him the runaround.'

'No?' said Cal grimly. 'Then what exactly were you doing with me last night?' He looked like a chess grand master who had announced checkmate in six moves.

Blaize lifted her eyes to his and then dropped them hurriedly. 'My relationship with Ned is none of your business,' she snapped.

'You made it my business,' grated Cal. 'Everything about you is my business. Besides, he's a policeman and he could be compromising himself.'

'Compromising himself?' repeated Blaize uncomprehendingly.

'By consorting with a possible criminal.'

The full force of what Cal was saying hit her like a ten-ton truck. 'Me?' she gasped. 'A possible criminal? How many times do I have to tell you——?'

'Save it,' said Cal. 'You can tell me as many things as often as you like and I guarantee I'll find it all great entertainment, but you can take it as read that I won't believe one word.

'I must say, I never imagined you having a police officer for a lover, although the fact that he's in the fraud squad seems extremely appropriate, given your characteristics.'

'Why, you——'

'Don't even bother trying to insult me,' said Cal wearily. 'Coming from you it's just plain hypocrisy.'

Blaize opened her mouth but no words came. She felt as though Cal had physically assaulted her. He had offered her the chance to tell the truth and she had hurled a pack of lies in his face.

He was looking away now, staring with extraordinary interest at the petrol pump. She suddenly knew with terrifying clarity that, for all his joking exterior, she had hurt him deeply. Had wounded that tough male pride by pretending that the previous night had meant nothing at all. She had done what she had set out to do, and the result was making her feel absolutely wretched.

There was nothing in the world she could say that would make him feel better towards her. And she knew now that, more than anything else, she wanted his respect, wanted simply to be plain Meg Bryan again, the object of his bantering affection.

But Meg Bryan was dead, she thought bitterly. And she had killed her.

Ned pulled open the driver's door and beamed at Blaize. 'Hello, love. I've brought you some chocolate. I know how it always perks you up.'

She felt herself blushing hotly under Cal's withering gaze as she took the bar Ned held out. Numbly she ripped the foil off the end and offered it to Cal. He looked as though she had handed him a scorpion. 'No, thanks, I think I'd be allergic to it,' he said grimly before turning his back on her.

She looked at Ned, who shrugged and took a piece. 'Look, Blaize, don't you think this——?'

'No, I don't,' she said sharply, forestalling him. She knew he wanted to tell the truth and dissolve the atmosphere that was thickening round them, but with that final remark Cal had pushed her too far. He could think what he liked, damn him.

The rest of the journey continued in silence until Ned stopped the Range Rover outside the block of flats where they lived. She opened the door and, slithering on the slush that had penetrated even as far as London, went round to Cal's side.

He wound down his window and looked at her silently.

'Goodbye, Cal,' she said stiffly. 'Thank you for getting me out of that snowdrift.'

'My mistake,' he said grimly.

She bit her lip. 'You're wrong about me, but it wouldn't matter what I said, you're so pigheaded you always have to believe you're right.'

'When it comes to you,' he snarled, 'I'm always right. All I have to do is jump to the worst conclusion I can think of and it generally turns out to fit exactly with what you've done.'

'This time you've jumped too far,' said Blaize softly. 'But you won't be told anything good about me, will you?'

'Tell me when you've joined a nunnery,' he grated. 'But until then as far as my good opinion's concerned you haven't a prayer.'

She pulled her eyes away from his and looked across at Ned. 'Goodbye, love. See you later.'

It was a victory of a sort, she thought, as she stood shivering, watching the Range Rover till it turned a corner out of sight, but a hollow one, for all that.

If only she hadn't had to pretend about who she was, then she wouldn't have had to go on lying and Cal would never have begun assuming the worst about her. The trouble was, they were both too proud to climb down.

She closed the door to the flat behind her and kicked off her shoes. It was heavenly to come home after all that had happened. She wandered around drawing the curtains, switching on the lamps and the central heating, doing everything she could to reassure herslf that she was safe once more in her own little cocooned world.

The first thing she wanted was a long, hot bath. Time seemed to slide past as she luxuriated in the water. It would be so easy to doze off. With a start Blaize woke up. How long had she been asleep? The water had gone cold and the tips of her fingers and toes looked like prunes. She let in some more hot and shampooed her hair.

Her hands stilled on the taps as the doorbell rang. Ned must have forgotten his keys again. Blast him. She reached for a terry robe and, soapy tendrils of hair licking her face, she got out of the bath and went to answer the door.

It was not Ned filling up the doorway, but Cal. Her first instinct was to slam the door in his face but he forestalled her, pushing his body through the gap. She stood back, suddenly conscious that all she was wearing was a loosely tied robe, and watched warily as he closed the door behind him.

He leant on it then, folding his arms across his chest and smiling slightly as he looked her up and down.

'I'm having a bath, if you don't mind,' said Blaize frostily.

'Before your brother comes back?' he asked idly.

Blaize's jaw dropped and she clutched the robe more tightly round herself. 'He told you?' she stuttered.

Cal shrugged. 'Of course he told me. Why shouldn't he? Ned is basically a very nice guy who thought he was doing his best for you. When I pointd out that he was just as bad at lying as his sister, he told me everything.'

'Just wait till I see him,' breathed Blaize. 'He's never betrayed a confidence before. And to you of all people.'

'Maybe he has a lot more sense than you give him credit for,' said Cal. And then, stepping towards her, he demanded, 'Why didn't you tell me the truth?

Heaven knows I gave you enough of an opportunity in
the car on the way home. Why, Blaize?'

'Because you made it so obvious you knew I was
lying,' said Blaize.

Cal blinked. 'Run that past me once again,' he said
slowly.

Blaize bit her lip. 'You're always so right about
everything,' she replied at last. 'You always have to
know everything. Why should I give you the pleasure
of notching up another correct answer? Another mystery solved? I'm fed up with you looking at me and
knowing exactly what I think.'

He raised an eyebrow. 'You do it to me,' he said
softly.

'That's an entirely different matter,' retorted Blaize
hurriedly. 'In any case,' she added defensively, 'I don't
always know what you're thinking. Sometimes you
close your eyes and then I can't see.'

'Women,' he muttered.

'What did you say?' demanded Blaize.

'I said, women,' said Cal. 'I'll never understand
them as long as I live. Especially you.'

There was a curious inflexion in his last remark and
Blaize looked at him sharply, but Cal had already
wandered through into the lamplit book-lined sitting-
room.

'Nice,' he remarked. 'Are all those books real, or
do they merely disguise a cocktail cabinet?'

'Certainly not,' snapped Blaize, unable to ignore his
needling and unnerved by his presence. 'And if that's
a hidden request for a drink you can think again. I
want you to go.'

He limped up to her and Blaize froze to the spot.
His fingers grasped the belt of her robe and pulled her

to him. 'But have you thought about what I want?' he whispered, bending his head and kissing her.

Blaize felt all the passion that he had kindled in her flame again. Then she felt her robe coming adrift and remembered how he had treated her that morning. She broke away with a little cry. 'That's all you ever think about, isn't it?' she said shakily. 'What you want? I suppose you think I should be flattered you're still interested in me. But you just treat people as things. You take them and use them and throw them away.'

Cal sat down in an armchair and smiled at her. 'I didn't know that it was possible to flatter you,' he said softly. 'I thought, as a beautiful woman, you regarded compliments as a sort of occupational hazard.'

'Don't change the subject,' said Blaize, blushing furiously at his remarks. 'You just think you can switch me on and off like some damn washing machine.'

He smiled. 'Somehow I must admit I never thought of you on the same lines as a consumer durable, but——'

'That's exactly how you do think of me,' retorted Blaize. 'And every other woman who catches your eye. You just switch them on, press all the right buttons and then, when you've had enough, swan off to your next conquest. I've met men like you before.'

'Ah, but have you slept with them?' said Cal, smiling infuriatingly.

'What do you think?' challenged Blaize, her jaw clenched.

'I think probably not,' he said softly. 'You lay a very good smokescreen, but really you're a one-man woman.'

'Well, you're certainly not him,' snapped Blaize, trying desperately to regain some self-control.

He looked at her disbelievingly. 'No?' he said lazily. 'Describe him to me, then.'

'My private life is none of your business,' yelled Blaize. 'Get out of my flat.'

'With pleasure,' he replied. 'As soon as you've finished your bath.'

'What's that got to do with anything?' she demanded.

He looked at his watch and then at her. 'Simply that you're coming out to dinner with me. You can come like that, of course—I think you look very fetching in pink terry towelling—but the restaurant staff might take a different view. Not a terrifically liberated bunch, waiters.'

Blaize stared at him. He must be completely crazy. 'Me come to dinner with you?' she managed, drawing her robe tight around her under his insolently knowing eyes.

He nodded. 'Correct. You win first prize in English comprehension.'

'I'm not going anywhere with you,' she said, absent-mindedly tying another knot in her belt. 'You're out of your mind.'

He sat back in the chair as though he owned it and everything else in the room, including her. 'On the contrary, you will come to dinner with me for several very good reasons.'

Blaize's curiosity got the better of her. 'Oh, yes? And what could they possibly be?' she said impatiently.

He grinned at her and she was suddenly irritated at her weakening resistance. 'I'm going to finish washing my hair and get dressed,' she snapped. 'And I want you to be gone when I get back.'

He slowly looked her up and down. 'Oh, I don't

know,' he said softly. 'I think I'll stick around in case you have any difficulty undoing all those complicated knots you've tied in your bath-robe. I used to be a boy scout, Blaize. I won badges for my knots.'

The underlying laughter in his voice was galling. She didn't trust herself to reply to him. Nothing would dent that arrogant armour of his. Contenting herself with a glare that would have stripped paint, she shot into the bathroom and slammed the door behind her.

He had been right too, damn him. The knots she had tied in her anger and frustration proved fiendishly difficult to undo. In the end she loosened the belt sufficiently to pull the whole robe over her head and then threw it furiously into a corner.

Why did he always have the same demoralising effect on her? Why could she never appear cool and in command when she was with him? He seemed to have this knack of reducing her poise to that of a gawky sixteen-year-old. She looked in the bathroom mirror and said sternly to her reflection, 'I'm not going to think about him. He is not worth it.'

But she knew he had not left the flat and his presence was, to say the least, disturbing. It was impossible not to think about him.

She thought of his lean, compact body and how he had given her so much pleasure, seemingly with so little effect on himself. Their time together seemed ages ago—had it really been only a few hours? She closed her eyes as if to block out the memory and stepped back in the gently perfumed, steaming water.

'You know, you really should lock your bathroom door. You never know who could come barging in.' Cal was behind her, leaning on the door-jamb.

'Get out,' Blaize gasped, trying ineffectually to cover herself with her hands.

'No,' he replied equably, reaching for the soap. 'It's much nicer in here. Want me to scrub your back?'

'Certainly not,' snapped Blaize, sliding deeper under the water as if the few remaining soapsuds could offer some protection against Cal's gaze. He trailed his fingers on the surface, brushing lightly over her breasts, and she stilled, her stomach knotting at his touch.

'Which button would you say I was pressing now, Blaize?' he asked gently.

'The remote control,' she muttered.

He laughed and took his fingers out of the water. 'You have exactly fifteen minutes to finish your bath and get dressed,' he said, picking up Blaize's bath-robe. He dried his hands on it, and then almost absentmindedly undid the knots she had had so much difficulty with. He dropped it on a chair and then turned to her. 'I'll go and make some coffee. Which way is the kitchen?'

Wordlessly she pointed and Cal made for the door. He paused as he left, and turned around. 'Here,' he said, grinning. 'Catch.' Something cold and hard slithered through her fingers and landed with a splash on her stomach. It was the soap.

CHAPTER SEVEN

BLAIZE wrapped her hair in a towel and pulled on her robe. The smell of good fresh coffee was drifting from the kitchen. She wandered through the doorway and watched Cal pour two cups.

He lifted the jug and stared at her over the curling wisp of steam. She wished suddenly that she were wearing more. . .like a bullet-proof vest.

She sipped the steaming liquid carefully, not daring to glance at him more than once or twice, painfully aware of the magnetism between them and the all-compelling reasons why she would not give in to it again. Could not afford to give in to it.

He looked at her steadily and then gazed pointedly at his watch. 'You have five minutes,' he said coolly. 'I must say, for a journalist, you have a very relaxed attitude to deadlines.'

'I'm not going anywhere with you,' repeated Blaize. 'I'm going to stay in, have baked beans on toast and watch TV.'

He shook his head. 'No. Sounds wonderful, but we'll do that another time.'

'I don't remember saying the word "we",' she said coldly.

'Must have been a slip of the tongue on your part,' he replied.

'Give me one good reason why I should go anywhere with you,' demanded Blaize.

He lifted his hand and began counting off on his

fingers. 'One, you are coming with me because I say so, and what I want I always get.'

Blaize opened her mouth but he was already on to his second reason. 'Two, your brother has finally plucked up courage to ask the girl of his dreams back to the flat this evening and he wondered if I could get you out of the way. Three——'

Blaize at last found her voice. 'He did no such thing,' she retorted, outraged. 'He wouldn't. He's my brother.'

Cal raised an amused eyebrow. 'He certainly did. And he certainly would. Why not? What's being your brother got to do with anything?'

'I mean,' said Blaize, trying against the odds to keep her voice even, 'I mean he tells me everything. Why should he tell you this and not me? All he had to do was pick up the phone.'

Cal took the coffee-cup from her trembling hand and set it on the counter. 'Don't take it too hard, Blaize. He was going to tell you, but your scheme of pretending you were engaged rather put the kibosh on his plans. I told him I was coming here and would pass the message on.

'How do you think I got him to admit he was your brother? He was doing his best to keep the story together, but the whole situation began to degenerate into some sort of bizarre farce when he found Marie waiting for him at headquarters.'

'Marie?' asked Blaize, bewildered.

'She's French,' said Cal helpfully. 'A sort of official translator working for the police. Very attractive, too.'

'He's never even mentioned her,' said Blaize limply.

'Probably worried you'd scare her off.'

Blaize glared at him. 'Thank you very much. Tell me——'

Cal looked back at his watch. 'No time, I'm afraid. I will answer all—well, nearly all—your questions in the restaurant. Meanwhile you have four minutes before I take you into your bedroom and start dressing you myself.'

Blaize pulled the towel from her head and ran her fingers through her hair. She was going to have the last word if it killed her. 'You said there were three reasons I should go out with you,' she said in as offhand a tone as possible. 'What's the third?'

He smiled at her. 'I suppose you want me to say it's the lure of your body, or the fascination of your razor-sharp mind. But unfortunately it's neither.'

Blaize's hand dropped from her hair and she stared at him. 'Don't tell me,' she said with icy sarcasm. 'You're after my Post Office savings account.'

'That'll do for a fourth,' he agreed. 'No. The third reason was simply that the restaurant we're going to has three stars in the Michelin guide and a soufflé I'm certain you would die for.' He glanced slyly at her. 'After sampling your cooking, I know just how much of a gourmet you are, Blaize.'

She glared at him. 'Are you suggesting I should come out with you merely because you're offering me the chance of a very good free meal?'

'Yes,' said Cal simply. 'Why not?'

'There has to be more to it than that,' said Blaize.

Cal turned away from her and put down the coffee-jug. 'Let's just say I want your company this evening.'

Blaize's heart leaped suddenly at his words. How did he manage to do this to her, to make her feel angry and flattered and all stirred up inside, all at the same time?

Her resolve weakened. It was impossible to refuse a man like Cal Smith. She was not even sure she wanted

to—not with the way she felt when he looked at her
the way he was doing now. Besides, she told herself
hurriedly, she could always get a taxi home if the
evening veered towards disaster. 'All right,' she said
with a sudden smile. 'I'll come.'

'Very kind of you, I'm sure,' said Cal, grinning.
'There's just one thing.'

Blaize stared at him impatiently. 'What now?'

'You still aren't dressed.'

She looked down at her robe, and then up at him,
the blood rushing to her face. 'Oh, you!' And, turning
tail, she fled to her bedroom.

She slid on her sexiest underwear, shivering at the
touch of the cold silk on her warm body, and unable
to explain to herself why she was worrying about her
lingerie when she had already resolved to keep Cal at
arm's length.

Then, clad only in a teddy and a pair of almost
invisible sheer stockings, she pulled open her wardrobe
door and stared in desperation at the contents. Beautiful dresses she had by the cartload—there was practically nothing else she liked to spend money on—but
tonight the one she chose had to be extra special.

It had to look stunning and yet at the same time she
had to appear as though she'd taken the minimum of
trouble over her appearance. She wanted to bowl him
over, not feed his ego. She pulled out dress after dress
and threw it on the bed. Talk about searching for the
impossible.

'Time's up.'

She whirled round to find herself practically in Cal's
arms. He had walked right up behind her and now he
was reaching out to steady her. At least, she thought
it was to steady her, but he didn't let go once she had
regained her balance. He merely drew her closer. 'I'm

trying to get dressed,' she muttered indistinctly, rattled by his closeness.

'I always thought clothes were a vastly over-rated invention,' he said, his fingers beginning to explore under the thin silk teddy. 'You only have to waste time taking them off.'

'Well, you're not taking any off tonight,' she said shakily, pulling away from him. 'You've just been lecturing me about how little time I have to get ready.'

Cal stood back with a smile, watching her with obvious amusement.

'How long have you been here?' she demanded, trying desperately to assert herself in a situation that seemed to be rapidly veering out of control.

'Long enough to wonder if you understood when I asked you out to dinner.' He smiled.

'What do you mean?' she asked, suddenly suspicious.

'Only that I intend to bring you back here afterwards, not take you on a three-year cruise ten thousand miles from the nearest dress shop.'

Blaize looked at the pile of clothes on her bed. Why did he always succeed in making her feel foolish? 'I lost one of my earrings,' she said as crisply as she could. 'I was searching for it.'

'Pearl drop, was it?' he asked softly.

She nodded dumbly. Cal reached out and touched the milky white drop on her right ear. Then his left hand brushed back her hair and he smiled down at her. 'Well, they're both here now.'

She breathed in deeply to try to control the jumpiness she felt at his closeness. But it was no good. He was drawing her closer again with that look on his face that made her want to run away from him and throw her arms around him, all at the same time.

'You wanted me to hurry up, didn't you?' she said, her voice sounding, to her ears, unnaturally high.

'Maybe I was wrong,' he whispered, burying his face in her neck.

She felt her senses reel as his kisses traced a path up to that soft secret place behind her jaw. 'Oh, Cal,' she whispered, 'Let's not go to dinner. Let's stay here.' She could hardly believe her own voice, but she knew she meant what she said.

She felt for Cal in a way that she felt for no man living. Feelings like this could not be denied by common sense. This attraction between them had to be special. Cal wanted her. He had said so. And he had come after her to the flat. She must be as special to him as he was to her.

She looked up at him with a pleading in her eyes that had not been there since she was nineteen years old. 'Please, Cal. We have so much to sort out. Now that I don't have to lie to you any more I want to tell you so much. Let's not go anywhere this evening.'

Was she mistaken, or did his body tense at her words? Then she felt him suddenly relax and drop his arms. 'We have to go out, sweetheart,' he sighed. 'We have to make way for Ned and Marie, remember?'

It was a reasonable excuse, but there was something definitely wrong. Cal was not the sort of man to let other people's plans head him off from what he wanted. Her heart lurched. Had she misread him? 'But——'

'No buts,' he smiled. 'And you're already into overtime.' He scanned the pile of clothes on the bed and, pulling out a black satin dress, held it up to her. 'Not bad,' he drawled. 'There's not much of it, but it leaves rather more to the imagination than anything else you've got.'

She grasped it wordlessly as he held it out to her.

He bent and kissed her cheek. 'Now put it on and hurry up. You've got thirty seconds.'

Blaize stood there holding the dress like a waxwork as he walked out. The utter nerve of the man. She had practically offered herself to him body and soul and then he simply hadn't wanted her. But he still felt like treating her as if she belonged to him. She looked down at the dress he had told her to wear and hurled it across the room. She was no man's property.

She ripped a silk frock from the pile and shrugged it over her head. It was red-gold, the exact shade of her hair, and it showed off her lithe body to perfection. She tore off her pearl drops and clipped on a pair of diamond earrings that had cost her a month's pay. Pearl drops were for good girls who did what they were told.

The sparkling facets added light to her face and she put her make-up on in record time. Stupid man. She would show him. She bent down, eased her feet into a pair of ridiculously impractical and breathlessly expensive gold sandals and stalked into the living-room.

'Well,' she told him, her chin up. 'I'm ready.'

'Really?' he drawled.

'What's the matter?' she demanded. 'Don't you like gold?'

'I'm sorry,' he said mockingly. 'I thought for a moment you'd decided to come out in your underwear.'

She glared at him. 'I've come out in a dress that I've chosen. It's that or nothing.'

He raised an eyebrow. 'Really?'

'You know exactly what I mean,' Blaize said impatiently.

Cal picked up his coat and, walking into the hall, took hers from the peg. He turned and, waiting for

her to catch up, held out his arm. 'Come along then.
We'd better hurry before you catch your death of
cold.'

Blaize fiddled with her heavy silver knife and looked
around at the quietly humming restaurant. The
warmth and civilisation was light-years away from her
first evening with Cal in the stable, and yet somehow
that had been by far the more relaxed experience.

They were both the same people, she reflected—or
were they? She was still attracted to him as to no other
man she had ever known, but so much had happened
in the last few hours that she could no longer even
guess how he felt about her.

Still, he had insisted on bringing her here and he'd
found out the truth about Ned; maybe he didn't think
she was so bad after all. If only she could completely
convince him that he had jumped to all the wrong
conclusions about her and that she wasn't the lying
journalist that he had supposed.

She studied Cal's face carefully as he spoke to the
waiter. He looked so tired, older somehow than the
man she had met in the snowdrift. God knew he'd
been under enough strain lately, but there was something else, a look in his eyes when he turned from the
waiter to her, that made her feel edgy and ill at ease.

There was something in the atmosphere between
them that she couldn't place. Something he had on his
mind. And it had to do with the way he had snubbed
her in her bedroom earlier. She was sure of it.

Cal had ordered quietly and efficiently and said
nothing as the waiter brought the wine and filled their
glasses. She twirled the stem of hers abstractedly and
nearly tipped it over when she raised it to his. 'To

truth,' he proposed, a glint in his eye belying his mild tone.

'Whatever that is,' countered Blaize, determined not to let him get the upper hand. She looked at his eyes again and then back at her glass. Something was definitely not right. 'You've not really brought me here as a favour for my brother, have you?'

'No,' he agreed quietly, 'I have not.'

Her heart thumped so heavily she felt he must have heard it. Was he going to accuse her of something else? Or had she completely misjudged his mood and was he about to make a pass? She smiled slightly. Maybe everything would turn out all right after all.

'Why are you smiling?' he asked softly.

She looked at him deadpan. 'I'm just wondering if it *is* my Post Office savings account you're after.'

'Not quite,' he replied.

The steel in his voice entered her heart. It was as though the floor had been whipped away from under her. She took a gulp of wine.

'Go on, then,' she said woodenly, trying hard not to let any emotions show. 'What are you going to accuse me of this time? Perhaps you think I helped myself to some family heirlooms while I was stumbling around your house in the middle of the night. Is that it?'

He rubbed his finger and thumb up and down the stem of his wine glass. 'You make me sound like some Gestapo character.'

'No,' she replied slowly. 'More like Torquemada in the Spanish Inquisition. He specialised in getting confessions from innocent people, didn't he? I'm surprised you haven't got the rack and the thumbscrews all ready.'

'Sorry,' Cal said mildly. 'I'm all out of thumbscrews.

And the only rack I can arrange in this place is made
of lamb.'

There was silence between them and he stared at
her clouded eyes. 'That was a joke, Blaize. You're
supposed to laugh.'

'I don't feel like laughing,' she said slowly, taking
another gulp of wine. 'Maybe you're not very good at
telling jokes this evening.' How could she have been
so foolish as to think he might care even a little bit
about her?

His hand was lying on the tablecloth and she longed
to grasp it, to say out loud how she felt about him, but
it was as though the air between them had iced over.

'Cal,' she said desperately, 'what's the matter?'

His eyes met hers and then looked away. 'Is there
something the matter?' he replied off-handedly.

'You know there is,' she said, trying hard to control
her voice. 'The atmosphere's all wrong and you know
it as well as I do. I don't know what I expected when I
agreed to come here, but when we're not at each
other's throats we. . .'

She stopped, afraid of revealing her emotions again
and yet, at the same time, afraid not to.

'We what?' he prompted. But there was no obvious
understanding in his eyes. His whole face had a closed-
in look and she couldn't tell what he was thinking.

'We get on quite well together,' she said lamely.
Then, looking up at him pleadingly, she said on impulse,
'Oh, Cal, you know as well as I do that there's some
sort of attraction between us. Something that you can't
deny. And now seeing you with that look on your face
I just don't know what to think any more. You remind
me of how I felt when I first met you——'

'When you thought I was a crook, you mean.' He

spoke slowly, without heat. 'Well, I told you not to trust me then, didn't I?'

'Trust you?' exclaimed Blaize unthinkingly. 'Of course I trust you. It's just. . .' She faltered, unwilling to give too much away to a man who could so easily hurt her. A man who had made her feel more alive than she had thought possible but who was now looking at her almost as if she were a complete stranger. 'It's just that, as I said, I don't always know what you're thinking.'

He looked at her thoughtfully. 'Well, that makes us even, sweetheart. You're like one of those Russian dolls. No matter how many layers I uncover there's always something concealed within. And you're wrong to trust me.'

'Am I?' Blaize whispered. 'I don't think so.'

'Yes, you are,' he said harshly. 'I don't trust you, and with this pensions scandal looming over me I can't afford to write you off as just a mystery lady I once spent a weekend with.'

'Which you would have done in normal circumstances,' said Blaize as steadily as she could, her heart frosting over. 'Just goodbye and thanks very much, and now please get out of my life?'

'Of course,' he replied calmly. 'Why not? It was, at times, a very enjoyable weekend. But I'm not looking for any long-term relationship, and besides, we're too different. You're an urban animal, Blaize. You like money and clothes and——' he paused '—fancy restaurants. While I'm——'

'A predator,' she supplied unsteadily, grasping the bottle and filling up her glass.

'Don't you think you're making rather large inroads into that wine?' asked Cal.

'Yes,' muttered Blaize fiercely. 'I've suddenly got a

terrible thirst.' She took another stiff belt of claret and then put her glass down on the table with great precision.

'So why have you brought me here?' she demanded. 'What do you want?'

'To know everything you know about the fraud in my company. Your contacts. Everything.'

So much for romance. Blaize felt as though she had fallen down a well. 'No,' she said flatly. They stared at each other across the table like mental gladiators. Her professional pride was at stake here and she was not going to compromise it. How dared he ask her for information he must know she regarded as confidential?

What a fool she had been to be secretly so pleased that Cal had asked her out, and then to find it was only because he wanted something from her. And what an idiot she was to feel so hurt. But she was not going to show how much. She breathed out as calmly as she could and said with forced brightness, 'Well, now we've disposed of that topic of conversation, do I get my dinner? Or was it merely conditional upon my coming across with all that information?'

Cal reached into his jacket and took out his wallet. Opening it, he extracted a piece of paper and laid it on the table before her. It was a cheque made out to her for a very large amount of money.

'You're trying to bribe me?' she whispered.

His face was hard, closed-in. 'It'll pay for an awful lot of silk shirts,' he said.

She looked down at the cheque again. The whole evening was turning into a nightmare. She grasped the wine bottle and splashed more wine into her glass.

For one moment she thought Cal was going to stop

her, but then he obviously changed his mind. Did he think she would be easier to bribe if she was drunk?

Drinking had never been her forte, but tonight she suddenly knew why some people never wanted to stop. Even so, it didn't seem to be doing a very good job of blotting out the awful reality that seemed to have taken over her life in the last few minutes.

She lifted her glass to her lips and mechanically read the figure on the cheque over and over again. The money he was offering would probably buy the factory that made the silk shirts. She remembered the night she had bandaged his hand, and felt her eyes begin to blur with tears.

'It's all yours, Blaize, if you tell me what I need to know,' he said coolly. 'I know you must have some very good contacts in the firm and I want to know who they are and what they told you. I've got to know.'

The tears were running freely down her face now. She could feel her mascara beginning to run, and she didn't care. She rose slowly to her feet and gripped the table. 'Money is all you understand, isn't it, Cal? Well, you don't understand me and you certainly can't buy me. Goddamn you to black hell for this.'

She picked up her glass and would have thrown it in his face if she hadn't realised that she had drunk all its contents.

Clutching it unsteadily, she turned from the table and reeled to the door. God, how much had she drunk? But before she reached the door, or even sprawled in front of it, Cal's hand was firmly under her elbow and she was being steered skilfully outside.

'Go away,' she threatened, 'or so help me, I'll give you a black eye.' She swung her arm back and tried in vain to shake him off, but his grip was like a vice.

Waiters hurried up to smooth away the scene, but

Cal stood solidly between them and Blaize. 'It's quite all right,' he told them as he dodged Blaize's ineffectual attempts to sock him on the jaw. 'The lady's suffering from terrible jet-lag. She's the boxing correspondent for the *Sporting Life*, you know.' He grabbed Blaize's arm. 'She's just been giving me her version of Mike Tyson's killer punch.'

Blaize, angry as a spitting cat, lashed out with her feet at his shins. 'She's quite an expert on Kung Fu, too,' added Cal, bending down and pulling her over his shoulders in a fireman's lift. 'So sorry we didn't have a chance to sample the Chateaubriand.' And, pushing a twenty pound note into the bemused waiter's hand, Cal carried Blaize outside and into a waiting taxi.

'Where to, guv?' asked the driver.

'Mayfair,' Cal answered shortly, pulling Blaize into the crook of his arm and imprisoning her wrists in one hand.

'I don't live anywhere near Mayfair,' she muttered, alcohol beginning to dull her reactions.

'No,' replied Cal. 'But I do.'

'I thought Blaize O'Halloran was a rough, tough reporter who could drink any normal man under the table,' said Cal, as he helped her up the thickly carpeted stairs of his apartment block.

'Well, you thought wrong on two counts,' Blaize replied dizzily as she leant against the wall and watched him fish out his keys. He pushed the door open and propelled her inside.

'First, I don't care much for alcohol,' she informed him owlishly, swaying in the marble entrance hall.

'Really?' he said drily.

'Really, truly,' she replied seriously. 'It fuzzes your

brain. You wouldn't believe how many stories I've got
by keeping sober in pubs. And second——'

'Yes?' He looked at her keenly.

'I am no longer a journalist. I was fired——' she
swayed and regained her balance '—this morning. As
a matter of fact. By Barney.' She looked at Cal to
make sure he was listening. Why were there two of
him? 'Barney's the man I told you was my husband.
Well, because I wouldn't dig the dirt on you, he sacked
me—divorced me, you might say. And you know
what? I——'

Her stomach lurched horribly. 'Oh God,' she muttered, 'I think I'm going to be sick.'

He opened a door. 'In here. Quick.' She fled into
the bathroom feeling utterly ashamed, but retained
enough self-control to lock the door. There was no
way she was going to let Cal see her like this. Minutes
passed like hours. She had never felt so utterly miserable in her whole life.

'Blaize, let me in.'

'Go away,' she whispered. How could he be so
insensitive?

'I've got something for you,' he persisted.

'If it's another cheque you know right where you
can shove it,' she called back bitterly.

'It's not a cheque, Blaize. That was an awful thing
to do to you. But it was necessary. I can explain.' His
voice was patient, reasonable.

'Even if you put your explanation in a suicide note,
I wouldn't read it,' she snarled.

'Stop fooling about, Blaize. You're ill, you drank
too much on an empty stomach and I should have
stopped you. Now open the door, or by God I'll break
it down.'

There was a note in his voice she could not ignore.

She opened the door, suddenly too tired to argue any further. He pressed a glass of water into her hand. 'Drink it.' She sipped it while he stepped to the shower and switched it on. He turned to her and ordered, 'Take your clothes off.'

She glared at him. 'Go to hell.'

He shrugged. 'OK. Don't say I didn't warn you.' And before she could even draw breath he lifted her up and thrust her bodily into the shower and closed the door.

The shock of the water was appalling. 'It's freezing,' she yelled.

'Turn up the hot, then,' replied Cal, standing with his back to the cubicle so she could not escape.

'You're a complete pig, you know that?' she yelled.

'Four-star, so I've been told,' he said as he opened the door. Whatever he was going to add died on his lips as he looked at her.

Her hair was snaking redly down her body now, the same colour as the soaked dress plastering her creamy body. Her wide grey-green eyes were framed by damp spiky lashes. The look on his face made her heart lurch, and then the invigorating effect of the shower began to take hold.

Wickedness and the desire for revenge bubbled up in her and, reaching out, she grabbed Cal's tie and pulled him into the shower. Water sluiced down his face and turned his immaculately cut grey suit to glistening black.

'You're a witch,' he said slowly, his hands travelling up her body.

'Well, at least it's an improvement on other names you've called me,' replied Blaize. 'Even though you did give me four stars.'

She swayed against him as he stripped the soaking

dress from her body and then slowly, almost methodically, began to soap her shining skin. It was almost more than she could bear, but cold rage at the way he had tried to bribe her was strong in her heart. It was too good a chance for revenge.

She slipped her arms around his waist and pulled him closer and then suddenly, glaring at him like a cornered cheetah, she brought her knee up in a vicious jerk. But he was too fast for her.

In one fluid movement he sidestepped her and, grabbing her arms, he lifted her up and pressed her against the tiled wall so that their eyes were dead level.

'You little vixen,' he yelled above the noise of the pounding water. 'And I was beginning to think I could trust you.'

'Trust!' she spat back. 'You don't know the meaning of the word. You tried to bribe me, goddammit. Do you know how that felt? To discover that someone you——'

'Someone you what?' he said softly.

She bit her lip. 'Just someone,' she corrected, adding, 'And to find that he has such a low opinion of you that he thinks he can buy you?'

Her feet were dangling at least a foot off the ground and his hands were biting into her arms. 'Let me go at once. I never want to see you or your lousy money again.'

He stared at her unblinkingly and then, as if he had heard nothing of what she had said, he leant forward and kissed her on the lips. Her whole body stiffened in shock but his mouth was warm on hers. Her heart felt as though it was in little pieces, but she could not ignore the demands he was making and she responded hungrily.

At last he drew away and let her down. There were

red marks on her arms where his fingers had bitten into her flesh, and he touched them gently. 'I'm sorry, Blaize. I didn't mean to hurt you.'

She felt close to tears now and shook her head blindly. 'It doesn't matter,' she said, watching him turn off the shower taps. Suddenly it seemed awfully cold and she began to shiver uncontrollably.

'Here.' He pulled a towel from behind the door and wrapped it round her. 'Go and make a hot drink while I get out of these clothes. I've got things I want to discuss with you.'

She stumbled to his shining kitchen, so different from the one in Oxfordshire. Her head was pounding from the amount of wine she had drunk. How could she have been so stupid? She thought of the hard lines in Cal's face and knew the answer to that immediately. He was just too much for her.

She grasped the chromium taps in the sink and twirled them on. Gratefully she bent her head to the rushing water and swallowed as much as she could.

This hangover would gradually go away. But how could she ever recover from the effect of a man like Cal Smith? She felt overwhelmed by him and ashamed of herself. How could she give in like that to a man who thought nothing of trying to bribe her?

Trying to knee him in the groin had been the only means of revenge open to her, and she had failed miserably. He had got the upper hand and she had given in to him. She hated him for it, but she hated herself more.

The hairs on the back of her neck prickled just as they had done light-years ago when she and Cal had first met in the snowdrift. He had padded into the kitchen as silently as a panther and she knew he was watching every move she made. Her hand shook as she reached for the tap and turned it off.

She dried her face silently and then opened a cupboard at random. The coffee was there on the bottom shelf and, trying hard to ignore his presence, she began spooning it into a jug.

'That makes ten spoonfuls.' Cal's voice was casual, almost matter-of-fact, and she nearly dropped the coffee packet.

'Oh, well,' she said as off-handedly as she could manage, 'I like it strong.'

He stepped close behind her. She could feel his breath on her neck and then his hand twining in her hair, turning her to face him.

'No other woman I know has ever attempted to do to me what you tried back there in the bathroom,' he said softly.

'I would have thought they would have been queueing up,' she muttered. His fingers tightened in her hair and she gasped. 'You tried to bribe me,' she said. 'You thought I would do anything for money.'

'Wouldn't you?'

'You really have a very low opinion of me, don't you?'

'What other conclusion could I have come to after your behaviour?' he said, his hand winding more and more tightly in her hair.

'You're hurting me,' she said unsteadily.

He loosened his grip. 'Maybe now you know how I feel,' he said softly.

'You?' said Blaize sarcastically. 'You don't feel anything. In fact I'm surprised your hand bled that night when you fell off the drainpipe. Thinking of it now, I wonder you don't have anti-freeze in your veins.'

His jaw clenched and Blaize waited for the verbal onslaught. But instead he sighed and looked at her patiently. 'Go and get dressed,' he ordered. 'I can't think straight with you looking like that. Get something out of my wardrobe and then we must talk. I'll make the coffee. You look as if you could do with some.'

Blaize stared angrily at him. 'The only thing I could do with right now is a machine gun.'

'What for?' he said coolly. 'So you could shoot yourself in the foot?'

'Well, I couldn't shoot you in the heart,' snapped Blaize. 'You haven't got one.' And then, turning on her heel, she ran swiftly out of the room.

CHAPTER EIGHT

BLAIZE perched on the edge of the sofa, dressed in one of Cal's silk shirts and a pair of chinos held up with a stripy tie. Her damp hair was the colour of a drenched fox and was already escaping from the handkerchief she had used to tie it up.

She looked round at the large, beautifully furnished room, and then at Cal leaning against the window. 'Well, there's one thing,' she ventured, uncertain of how to break the icy tension between them but determined to try.

He raised an eyebrow at her and she ploughed on, 'At least it's warmer than your house in Oxfordshire.'

He padded over to the sofa opposite her and sat down. 'Don't be so fatuous, Blaize. I've got three million things on my mind at the moment and none of them involves central heating.'

'Pity,' she said coldly. 'Your bloodstream could do with some.'

He looked at her stonily. 'There's only one cold-blooded creature in this room and that's you.'

'Oh, yes?' she retorted furiously. 'You're the one who's guilty of attempted bribery and corruption. How do you think that's going to look in open court? I'm beginning to think you were involved in that fraud after all. You get all the money and the directors take all the blame. Very neat.'

'You're being absurd,' he said.

'Am I?' she replied bitterly. 'What about that cheque you tried to give me? How are you going to explain that away?' She banged her mug on the floor. 'You must be absolutely stark staring mad if you think you can get away with this, Cal.'

He looked at her coolly. 'In the first place, you have no proof. What cheque exactly are you talking about?'

'The cheque you tried to bribe me with,' said Blaize impatiently.

'Oh, that cheque. Destroyed, I'm afraid.'

'And in the second place?' demanded Blaize, determined not to be unnerved by his bland assurance.

'The second is a bit more difficult.'

'I might have known it,' she said. 'Save your breath. I don't want to hear any crummy excuses. I'm leaving.' She began to rise.

'You are doing no such thing,' he said. 'You will stay where you are and you will listen to what I have to say.'

'Make me,' she challenged.

'If I have to, I will,' he said. 'And you know it. But I think you'd prefer to stay there of your own free will. After all, think of the great story you might be missing.'

Blaize sat down again. 'There is that,' she said icily. 'And if I can help put you behind bars then so help me, I will.'

He looked at her for a few moments as if trying to make up his mind about something. 'Well?' she prompted.

'You are not going to like this, Blaize.'

'That I can believe. I can't see myself liking any pathetic excuse you're going to come up with.'

'I offered you the cheque,' he said steadily, 'because we rather thought you might be mixed up in all this.'

'You did what?' Blaize gripped the cool linen seat

cushion of the sofa. A horrible sense of unreality
began to grip her.

'There were several things we couldn't understand
about the case. The tip-off that my crooked colleagues
were to be arrested. That sort of thing. And when I
realised who you were, it all seemed too good to be
true—so pat that you should be there at all. So I
agreed to bait a trap. If you took the money you would
also be agreeing to give us information which might
prove very useful. And if not——' he shrugged
'—then, by showing you had some morals, at least
over accepting cash, you would probably be in the
clear.'

'Ned,' she breathed. 'Was Ned part of this?'

'No,' said Cal. 'He protested your innocence but
saw that it would be better all round if it were proved
conclusively.'

'But I could have just pretended to take it,' said
Blaize. 'It would have made a brilliant story. You
would have been down in print as being completely
corrupt. And what would you have done then?'

He looked down into the bottom of his mug. 'Well,
there always was that risk, but I was banking on the
fact that you are such an appalling liar. You can't
pretend anything without it being written all over your
face. Also, if it had gone as far as the newspaper the
police would have just stepped in and explained.'

'So I've passed your test,' said Blaize slowly.

'If you want to put it like that, yes,' he replied.

'Do I get an apology?' she demanded coldly.

'What for?'

She stared at his cool expression. 'What do you
mean, what for?' she burst out. 'For having the gall to
treat me like a bloody criminal, that's what for.'

His eyes never wavered from her face. 'You treated

me like one, Blaize. And I haven't noticed you apologising.' He leant across and grasped her hand. 'Or complaining, for that matter.'

She thought of the night she had spent with him and wrenched her hand away. 'Don't touch me!' she yelled.

'Why?' he said softly. 'Are emotions too much for you to handle?'

'Don't talk to me about emotions,' she stormed. 'The only ones you experience are probably when you contemplate spending money.'

Her head was pounding and she felt sick and dizzy from the remains of the alcohol in her system. She stood up suddenly like a child at a party. 'I want to go home,' she said. She put a hand up to her face. 'Why do I feel so awful?'

Cal sprang up and moved to her side. 'You're tired and hung over, that's why. And you haven't had anything to eat for hours. You're in no state to go anywhere.'

Blackness seemed to be folding over her eyes. 'Do you know, Cal,' she said, 'I think——'

She took a step towards him and then everything went black. But he caught her before she fell, and, lifting her in his arms, carried her to the bedroom.

The nightmare, when it came, was the same as all the other ones that had plagued her sleep since she was nineteen. But this time, when she cried out, a voice answered her. A soothing voice.

'I didn't know,' she yelled. 'I didn't know.'

'Blaize, wake up.'

Her eyes started open and she found herself sitting bolt upright in bed with Cal's arms around her. She stared at him, still not fully awake. 'Tell him I didn't know,' she pleaded wildly. 'Tell him.' And then the realisation of reality struck and she burst into tears.

Cal pulled her close and held her until her sobs subsided. Then, reaching out on to the floor, he handed her a box of paper tissues. 'Here, take this.'

Wordlessly she pulled out a wodge of tissue and wiped her eyes. 'Want to talk about it?' he said gently.

She blew her nose noisily and hiccupped. 'I'm just a journalist, remember? I routinely tell secrets to millions of people before breakfast. Why don't I just write a piece about my private life for a change and you can read about it in the paper?'

Cal's lips twisted. 'I think you'd find that a bit difficult, Blaize. You've been sacked, remember?'

Another sob forced its way up her throat but Blaize forced it back. He shook her gently by the elbow. 'Come on. Tell me about your nightmare. We've really nothing to hide from each other now.'

'That's true,' muttered Blaize. 'You've made it perfectly obvious how little you like me. It's just my body you're interested in.'

Cal shook up the pillows behind him and then lay back, drawing Blaize into the crook of his arm. 'I want to go home,' she said weakly.

'No, you don't,' replied Cal. 'Why should you when I'm here?'

Blaize opened her mouth but he continued smoothly, 'Besides, this bed's much more comfortable than that thing in your flat that looks like a broken-down orange box.'

'It's a futon,' she corrected, her fingers unconsciously entwining with his.

'You said it,' he remarked.

The silence stretched between them, a companionable silence that seemed to last so long she thought

Cal must have fallen asleep. But then the feeling that she must unburden herself, even if no one was listening, was overwhelming.

'I've had that nightmare since I was nineteen years old,' she said softly, remembering. 'Ever since I stormed out of the house after a row with my father.'

Cal's fingers tightened around hers. So he wasn't asleep, just letting her speak in her own time. 'What happened?' he asked.

Blaize lay back in Cal's arms. 'I had the biggest, bitterest shouting match you've ever seen or heard, and it was all over my first love-affair,' she said slowly. 'I suppose it's quite funny really when I remember how you accused me of two-timing my non-existent husband.'

Cal's hand tightened around hers and she tried to smile.

'So why the nightmares?' he said softly.

She sat up suddenly and looked at him. 'Remember I told you I ran away from home once?'

He nodded. 'Yes, I wondered about that, I must admit.'

'Well, I was nineteen years old and completely bowled over by a man who seemed to me to be the best thing since sliced bread.'

Cal snorted. 'Very romantic turn of phrase,' he muttered.

She looked at him askance, a new understanding in her eyes. 'You're jealous,' she said wonderingly.

'I am not jealous,' grated Cal. 'What happened to him? Go stale on you?'

Blaize opened her mouth to reply but Cal forestalled her. 'What was his name, anyway? Not that I'm really interested.'

'Sean,' said Blaize, grinning in the darkness. 'He

turned out to be a complete snake who thought I was a heaven-sent opportunity to cheat on his wife.'

'I'd like to wring his neck,' muttered Cal.

'So did I, at the time,' said Blaize. 'It was absolutely awful when I found out. I just couldn't believe that anyone could be so charming, could say all those things to me, and that it was all a complete sham. I've never really trusted anyone ever since.'

'And you went back to your father's after Sean showed his true colours?' asked Cal gently.

She shook her head. 'I tried to but he wouldn't have me in the house. Said I'd blackened my mother's memory. Real Victorian religious guilt trip. The whole bit.' Her voice wobbled at the memory.

'Is that what all the nightmares are about?'

'Yes,' she said slowly. 'Because he was so angry. I've never seen anything like it. It was terrible. Frightening. When I think of it now I realise maybe it was because he was so upset, and he blamed me for it. And then I got angry too. Completely lost my temper and said a lot of things I didn't mean. Awful things. That was it then.

'He really did show me the door and throw my things out after me, and there was me begging for him to listen and him not hearing a blind word. I hated him then. Afterwards I was just too proud to back down. And now it's probably too late.'

'It's never too late,' said Cal. 'You should go home soon and make peace with your father and yourself.'

Blaize opened her mouth to protest and then thought again of what Cal had said. The idea of ending a feud that now seemed silly and pointless was like a load falling from her back.

She sighed. 'Yes, I think you're probably right.'

Cal leant down and kissed her, his hand smoothing

away the tears that slid across her cheeks. 'Go to sleep, Blaize. You're all right now, I promise.'

She attempted to smile and closed her eyes. It was true, she was really very tired.

The grey early morning filtered through the half-open curtains and Blaize woke with a start. Where on earth was she? One glance at Cal lying by her side answered that question. He was fast asleep. As she looked at his supremely contented face the events of the night before came flooding back.

She thought of the cheque Cal had tried to give her and her heart fell. And her stupid nightmares. Why on earth had she told him about Sean? She had exposed her innermost secrets to a man who had tried to bribe her.

All she was doing was repeating history. Surely she couldn't trust a man who behaved like that, whatever excuse he came up with.

She slid carefully out of the bed and padded into the kitchen to make some tea. The telephone answering machine was on the counter and its light was winking. Without even thinking what she was doing she pressed the button and listened to the messages. There was only one. 'Cal, it's Sophie Harrison. I left you a message in Oxfordshire but you obviously haven't got it. I do need you rather desperately. Can you come round?'

Blaize switched off the machine and stared at it grimly. Her instincts had been right. She was just about to be made a fool of, all over again. What on earth was she doing in Cal's flat letting herself be messed around like this? Cal didn't give two hoots for her.

He had practically said so. She snorted as she

remembered the words that had seared across her brain: 'Parts of the weekend were quite enjoyable'.

Infuriating man. He obviously had no shortage of female company. So why did she have to help massage his already inflated ego?

She had to get out of here and fast. She was no rich man's toy. She was a career woman, and, by God, she was going to show him a thing or two.

Blaize strode into the bathroom to get her dress. It was still damp from the night before but she pulled it on furiously. There was no way she was going to get back into Cal's clothes again. The very touch of them would burn her skin.

She blushed as she remembered how Cal had undressed her. What a state to get into. What had she been thinking of? She thrust her feet into her sandals, grabbed her coat and bag from the chair in the hall where she had dropped them the previous night, and ran out of the flat as if it were on fire, instead of just her heart.

The porter at the desk in the foyer raised his eyebrows at the sight of Blaize, wild-haired and wild-eyed, marching downstairs in the clothes she'd worn the night before. 'Don't even think it,' she told him menacingly. 'I know exactly what's running through your mind and you can forget entirely any sordid ideas of what I may have been up to.'

'Yes, miss,' said the porter, subdued by the authority in her voice.

'And you can get me a taxi, please,' she added, a muscle thudding in her cheek. The porter all but clicked his heels.

'Certainly miss. Right away.'

* * *

Blaize felt exhausted as she put her key in the lock. The last few days had just been too much. 'Ned!' she exclaimed, seeing him standing by the kitchen door.

He grinned sheepishly at her. 'Did you have a good night?'

She glared at him. 'You must be joking. Cal set me up with some stupid test to see if I was immune to bribes and you, I discover later, know all about it.'

Ned backed into the kitchen. 'It wasn't my idea,' he said soothingly.

'No,' she replied. 'I can guess where that came from.'

'Really?' said Ned. 'I didn't think you had met my boss.'

'Your boss?' Blaize banged her handbag down on the kitchen counter. 'What's he got to do with anything?'

'He was the one who insisted Cal tried to bribe you. You should have heard the row. Cal really stuck up for you, you know.'

'Did he?' said Blaize unbelievingly. 'I don't believe you.'

Ned grinned. 'He said no crook in their right minds would try to use such an appalling liar as you. Apparently the top brass wanted him wired for sound to tape your conversation.'

Blaize's eyes widened. Was the whole of the previous night on tape? 'And was he?' she asked. God, what had she said to him over dinner last night?

'I've no idea,' Ned admitted. 'They wanted me out of the way, that's for sure. I've been put on other duties.'

'But, Ned, that's terrible. They can't push you about like that.'

He shrugged. 'Doesn't really matter. My honesty

isn't in question. They just didn't want me compromised by family loyalties. And you're in the clear, obviously, otherwise you wouldn't be here, so there's nothing to worry about.'

'God, what a mess,' Blaize sighed. She brightened suddenly. 'What's all this I've been hearing about Marie? I want to know everything. I hope she's beautiful and nice and kind.'

Ned grabbed his coat and grinned. 'I'll tell you later. You'll really like her. Must go or I'll be late for work.' And he was gone.

Blaize looked at the phone. Perhaps, if she asked Barney very nicely, he would give her her job back. However much of a pig he was, he was better than any other national news editor. Besides, no other paper would take her without all the detailed background to the fraud case, and Barney had that locked in his personal file.

If she was going to be truthful with herself, she wanted to go back simply because of Cal. She wanted the inside story on exactly what was going to happen to him.

As she stared at the phone it began to ring. She snatched the receiver up. 'Barney,' she said joyfully.

'Wrong,' came the voice she knew too well. 'Try again.'

'Cal,' she whispered.

'Correct,' he grated. 'What the hell are you playing at? What do you mean by running out on me like that?'

'I didn't run out on you,' she said icily. 'I've come home. That's all. This is where I live. Why should I stay where I'm not wanted? And after all, you'll be so busy today, you won't have any time for me.'

'Cut the "poor little me" act, Blaize; it doesn't suit you.'

'All right,' agreed Blaize. 'In plain language then. I don't trust you, Cal Smith. You take me out to dinner and try to trap me, while recording every damn word I say. You didn't tell me that last night, did you?'

'There wasn't much chance,' said Cal. 'In any case, I thought it might upset you.'

'Well, how thoughtful,' replied Blaize bitterly.

'Come on, Blaize, you're over-reacting. Why don't you meet me for breakfast? Lots of carbohydrates are good for hangovers.'

'I am not hung over!' screamed Blaize, clutching her pounding forehead. 'Why don't you meet bloody Sophie for breakfast if you're so desperate for company? She certainly is.' And she banged down the phone and pulled out the plug.

She was not going to speak to that man ever again. Not if it killed her. How dared he say she had a hangover when it was all his fault? And wearing a damp dress in freezing temperatures didn't help. Perhaps she had flu coming on. She clutched her head and wandered into the bathroom. Where had Ned put the aspirins?

The middle of the newsroom in late afternoon, just as everyone was gearing up for production of that night's newspaper, was not the best place to plead her case, but Barney had not been interested in meeting her for lunch. Hadn't seemed interested in meeting her at all. Blaize clasped her hands and tried not to show her nerves. Everyone else in the offfice, while pretending to be scorchingly busy, was drinking in every word of this conversation. And the last thing she needed was a

cynical audience for her attempt at sweet-talking her
way back into a job.

Blaize gritted her teeth. She would just have to do
her best. Barney was obviously determined to make
things as difficult as possible for her. Her refusal to
write that story about Cal had clearly riled him much
more than she thought.

'Why should I give you your job back?' he
demanded.

'Because I'm the best reporter you've ever had,'
said Blaize.

Barney raised his eyebrows. 'Such modesty. But
then, that was never one of your problems, was it?'

'You don't need modesty,' replied Blaize. 'You need
me.' She sighed. 'Come on, Barney. This fraud case is
coming up and no one else in the office knows as much
about Cal Smith as I do. Plus I have the best contacts
book in this office, and without it how else are you
going to get all those celebrity interviews that I do so
well?'

Barney turned from his terminal and looked at her.
'All the reporters in this office are just as competent
as you, Blaize. No one is indispensable, you should
know that by now.'

He leant over the desk to yell at his deputy and then
turned back to her. 'I'll tell you straight, Blaize, you're
a damn good reporter, but I'm not used to my staff
telling me they're not going to write what I want.'

Blaize thought of how he had wanted her to write
about her weekend with Cal and a crushing retort
sprang to her lips. Then she thought of all the unpaid
bills in her bag and bit her lip. 'I'm sorry, Barney,' she
said meekly. 'It won't happen again.'

He looked at her for a few minutes and then went

back to his terminal. 'Good,' he said. 'See that it doesn't.'

'You mean I'm hired again?' breathed Blaize.

He grinned at her. 'Actually, you were never officially fired. I couldn't be bothered with the paperwork. Besides, I knew you'd be back.'

Blaize thought of all the humble pie she had just been forced to eat. Rage boiled up in her. 'You——'

'Yes, I know,' nodded Barney. 'It's part of the job title.'

The magistrates' court was a Victorian gothic nightmare in stone. It was also extremely chilly and Blaize blew on her fingers to keep warm. How dared Barney send her here?

It was like punishment duties. She gritted her teeth. She hadn't been to a magistrates' court since she was a cub reporter and she felt the humiliation deeply—even if it was the committal hearing for the directors of Cal's company.

Every other paper would be taking agency copy, but not Barney. 'Something could happen, Blaize,' he had said, 'and I want you there.'

She sighed. With any luck the case would be called soon. As a preliminary hearing it would all be over in a few minutes. Maybe she could get back to the office before lunch and start soft-soaping her way back into Barney's favour.

She turned on her heel to enter the court when she saw Cal. He was deep in conversation with a barrister, but what really stopped Blaize's heart was the beautiful blonde by his side.

It had been two days since they last spoke. But Cal, as she knew to her own cost, was a notoriously fast worker. Was this Sophie, who had needed Cal so desperately in her answering machine messages? Or was it someone else entirely?

Blaize looked at the woman and felt a stab of hot jealousy. She had spent most of yesterday trying to ring Cal to apologise.

No wonder he hadn't been answering his telephone.

Cal raised his head and their eyes met. He said something to the woman and the barrister and then began walking towards her. Blaize, her hand on the door to the court, wanted with all her soul to walk inside, anywhere so long as it was away from him, but it was no use. She was rooted to the spot.

He walked right up to her as if he owned her. She wanted to step back but the wall was at her back. He was wearing a charcoal suit and the tie of a famous guards regiment. His eyes were soft, amused, and she tried to stop feeling as though she could fall into their brown depths.

'Back at the old game, I see,' he said.

'Some of us have to earn a living,' she replied shortly, trying desperately to keep a rein on her nerves.

'So that's what you call it,' he said mildly. 'And I thought you were just hanging round watching other people's lives go by.'

Blaize glared at him and, looking pointedly at the blonde, retorted, 'I see you've been living down to your reputation. And don't tell me she's only interested in your beautiful brown eyes.'

His expression became if anything more amused. It was infuriating. 'A personal compliment already,' he drawled. 'I'll write it down in my diary.'

Blaize pursed her lips. He was obviously not going to tell her who the blonde was. And she was not going to ask.

He put his hand under her chin and tipped her face
up to his. 'The green-eyed monster really has got you,
hasn't it?'

'I don't know what you mean,' she struggled. 'Let
me go.'

'Jealousy, Blaize. That's what's eating you,' he said.

'Let me go,' Blaize repeated.

'You have such beautiful lips,' he said. 'Do you
think I'll get arrested for contempt of court if I kiss
them?'

'Why don't you kiss your blonde instead?' spat
Blaize and, wriggling from his grasp, shot into the
courtroom, his laughter ringing in her ears.

Her sudden entrance into the hushed room caused a
mild stir. Blaize smiled weakly at the presiding magis-
trate and sat down quickly on the Press bench.

All her instincts had been right. The hearing took
no more than a few minutes, just long enough for the
four men in the dock to enter their pleas and for them
to be given bail.

Three pleaded guilty and Blaize stifled a yawn as
she made a note of their names and addresses. She
already had all this stuff, but you could never be too
careful. The fourth man, John Harrison, pleaded not
guilty. Harrison. Where had she heard that name
before? Her eyes widened in surprise. He had the
same surname as Sophie. She nudged the agency
reporter next to her. 'Know anything about his background?' she asked, ultra-casually.

'Not much,' he replied. 'Saw his wife outside earlier.
Spectacular bonde. Sophie, I think her name is.'

Blaize nodded her thanks and edged out of the
courtroom. A tall figure rose from the back of the
court and held open the door for her. 'Going my way?'
asked Cal.

'I hope not,' retorted Blaize.

'Oh, but I think you are,' he replied mildly, putting his hand under her arm. She tried to shake him off, with no success.

'It's no use, Blaize,' Cal said conversationally. 'Drunk or sober, you won't be able to get away from me. Unless,' he added with a glint in his eye, 'I decide to let you go.'

'You are the most impossible man I've ever met,' Blaize hissed, conscious that people were looking at them.

'Another compliment,' he remarked. 'Two in one day! I think you must be getting soft in your old age.'

The bitter December wind stung her face as they left the court by a side door and got into a dark Rolls-Royce waiting at the kerb.

Cal leant forward and spoke to the chauffeur. 'Back to town, Roberts, but as slowly as you like.' He closed the glass partition and leant back in his seat. 'Alone at last,' he murmured. 'How romantic.'

Blaize looked out of the window at the slow river of traffic and said nothing. His nearness was too disorientating. She swallowed and tried to breathe slowly but it was no use. Her heart seemed to be beating out some Latin American rhythm and her brain had gone to lunch. How was it that one man could have this effect on her?

She felt his hand on her shoulder, turning her gently but firmly to face him.

'We have a lot to talk about,' he said.

'Do you have your tape running?' replied Blaize steadily. 'Or would you like me to use my shorthand?'

His eyes sparked with annoyance. 'The tape was not my idea, Blaize, but it clinched your innocence in the eyes of some very suspicious policeman.'

'How long did you leave it running?' she demanded.
'I expect you had a really good laugh over my antics
when you took it to your pals at the station.'

Cal sighed. 'I switched it off in the restaurant, if you
must know. I thought it was a completely stupid idea,
but I had to show everyone else that you were as
innocent as I knew you to be.'

'Thanks very much,' said Blaize dully.

Cal's fingers stroked her cheek. 'Stop fighting me,
Blaize. You can't win.'

Oh, how she loved the feeling of him being so close
to her. She wanted so much to close her eyes and let
him take control, let everything just slip away.

'Come back to Oxfordshire with me,' Cal urged.

Blaize swallowed. 'I'm an urban animal, remember?
You're not looking for any long-term relationship,
remember? It was a nice weekend in parts, remember?
And in normal circumstances you would have just
written me off as being merely a part of life's rich
tapestry. Wouldn't you?'

Had it been only a few days ago that he had said
those things to her? It was as if they had been festering
in her soul for a lifetime. She brought up each painful
word and flung them back at him with deliberate
venom. His eyes hardened and he withdrew his hand
as if he had been holding a snake.

She glared at him, hurting more inside with every
word she said. 'What do you want this time, Cal? My
body? Are you going to pay me by cheque over the
dinner-table every Friday night?'

He raised his hand to slap her then, and she gasped
at the realisation of what he was going to do, tears
spurting out of her eyes. Then he let his hand fall back
limply.

'I've never hit a woman in my life before and I'm

not going to start now,' he rasped, 'but, by God, Blaize O'Halloran, you've come closer than any woman alive to making me lose my self-control.'

The car had stopped at traffic lights. Blindly she felt for the door-handle and flung herself out of the car, hurrying down the icy pavement, completely heedless of where she was going. She looked back at one point, wondering against reason if Cal was following her, but in the press of early Christmas shoppers she could see nothing.

CHAPTER NINE

BLAIZE struggled through the crowds to the nearest Tube station. The hot air was like a blast from hell after the icy winds on the street and she began to shiver uncontrollably as she pushed her way on to the crowded train. She felt ill and tired and at near breaking point after her encounter with Cal.

She did not know what to think about her relationship with him. She wanted so much the comfort she knew he could give her. But it was too frightening to contemplate giving that much of herself to one man. Especially a man like Cal. What if he did just want to begin where they had left off? What if after another weekend he would just sweetly wave her goodbye and forget all about her? What if? What if?

And, more gallingly, what about Sophie? She thought of the humiliation of meeting Sean's wife and swallowed hard. She was not going to go through that again. Not ever.

The questions and words whirled around and around in her brain infuriatingly. It was almost as if she had lost the ability to think at all. The only sure thing in her life was work. Perhaps if she threw herself back into that she would begin to put the events of the last few days in a more reasonable perspective. Perhaps.

She sighed and dragged her aching body out of the Tube train and along to the office. A bout of flu on top of everything else that had happened to her seemed so unfair. She would just have to ignore it and hope it went away.

Back at the office she stared at her computer screen for a long while. Cal and Sophie. Sophie and Cal. They had looked so good together. So right, somehow. How could she ever imagine that a man like Cal would prefer her over anybody else, especially a woman so stunningly beautiful as Sophie Harrison?

What did Sophie mean to him? 'I need you desperately.' That had been the message on Cal's answering machine. Just how desperately had she needed him? Was she two-timing her husband? Had she been mixed up in the fraud too? Maybe she and Cal had planned it all together, making sure others, including her husband, took the blame and went to prison while they were left free to enjoy the missing pension funds.

Blaize ran her hand abstractedly through her hair. Cal wouldn't have plotted something like that. He wasn't dishonest. He couldn't be. She thought of the night they had spent together and the cheque he had attempted to give her and almost cried aloud in her anguish. What was she going to do?

'Blaize!'

She looked up to see Barney scowling at her from a distance of about six inches. She instinctively moved back. 'There's no need to shout, Barney,' she said, trying to recover her composure.

'Shout?' he retorted exasperatedly. 'I could have put an atom bomb under you and you wouldn't have noticed. I've been trying to get your attention for the last five minutes and you've paid me as much attention as a used hankie. I thought you'd died.'

'Well, I've come back to life,' snapped Blaize. 'What do you want?'

Barney raised an eyebrow and then, straightening up, said very softly, 'Oh, nothing much.'

Blaize, surprised by his gentle tone, looked up.

'Nothing, that is,' said Barney, his tone hardening until his voice became like raw vodka pouring over gravel, 'except some good work out of you.' The office quietened, everyone looking across at them, glad they weren't in Blaize's shoes.

She stared back at him as coolly as she could, and resisted the urge to run her tongue over her dry lips. 'Fair enough,' she replied. 'Any ideas?'

Barney stared at her, his eyes narrowing until they were like little slits and then blinking open suddenly. 'Yes,' he barked. 'What about that profile?'

'Profile?' repeated Blaize, knowing with horrible certainty what he wanted.

Barney sighed. 'The profile I asked you to do of Cal Smith. "My Weekend At His House", et cetera et cetera. God knows we paid you enough in advance expenses to go there. I got the bill for your abandoned car this morning. And if you don't want to end up paying for it yourself, my girl, I'd get writing now.'

Blaize bit her lip. 'Yes, Barney. All right.' He watched her begin to tap her keyboard, and then, nodding slowly, walked away and left her in peace.

A profile, Barney had said. And a profile was what he was going to get. But maybe not quite the hatchet job he had expected. She sighed and rubbed her forehead with the back of her hand. Why did she feel so hot? Her head was pounding again but she looked down at the keyboard and began doggedly tapping out the first words. And to her surprise once she began there was no stopping.

All her pent-up thoughts about Cal came tumbling out. His magnetism, his humour, his love of the simple life. What he had said about his family. Conor. Blaize smiled as she remembered how she had been so afraid of the big soppy dog.

Eventually she sat back with a sigh and pressed the send button. She got up and went to see Barney. 'Well?' he glared at her, not willing to be the first one to make amends.

'I've written it,' said Blaize simply. 'Two thousand words, and rather good ones if I say so myself.'

Barney's expression softened a little. 'That was quick. Well done.' He pressed a button on his terminal and called up the story. Blaize watched him expectantly as he began to read.

'What the hell is this?' he roared, stabbing his finger at the screen.

'It's a computer,' said Blaize sarcastically. 'You file stories on it.'

'I mean this rubbish,' he yelled, pointing at her story. 'This is a newspaper, not a fan magazine.'

Blaize reddened. 'I can't help it if I like the guy,' she said.

'Like him?' roared Barney. 'This is a no-holds-barred love-letter!'

Blaize's face paled. 'Don't be ridiculous,' she stammered. But it was true. She realised with blinding certainty that Barney's usual over-the-top criticism had, for once, been bang on.

'I don't want this rubbish,' he continued. 'Our readers simply aren't interested in the exact colour of his eyes or the name of his bloody dog. They want to know how many girlfriends he's had. We're going to use a big picture of him with that blonde he was with at the court this morning.'

'How did you know about her?' gasped Blaize, suddenly feeling as though she had fallen down a lift shaft.

'The local Press agency filed,' said Barney, adding brutally, 'Unlike you. According to them, Cal Smith and this woman, Sophie something or other, seemed as close as it is possible to get in public. We've got a great picture of them arriving at the trial. He's supporting her arm, smiling down at her. Lovely shot. Of course, she played the loyal wife when her husband was given bail, and your Mr Smith certainly kept a low profile after that, but it's definitely worth a story.'

Blaize stood speechlessly as Barney hammered out his instructions. 'I want all you can get on Sophie Harrison. Is she going to ditch her crook of a husband for Cal? Has she moved into his house yet? Are they going to get married? Get her on the telephone. I want quotes. Good ones.' He nodded curtly and began moving away to the picture desk.

The word 'married' hit Blaize like a cruise missile. Was it obvious to everyone that there was something between Sophie and Cal? She was damned if she was going to write a story about their burgeoning romance. The profile she had written just served to show what a blind fool she had been. Her head pounding, she smashed her hand on the keys of Barney's terminal and saw her words disappear. Barney turned around in surprise and, without thinking, she unplugged his keyboard and heaved it at him.

He ducked and it smashed against the wall, narrowly missing the foreign desk. 'And I thought Kuwait City was bad,' the foreign editor remarked, picking shards of plastic out of his hair.

But no one was bothered about the foreign editor. Barney took one step towards Blaize and then stopped, with his fists clenched. 'You're fired,' he yelled. 'And this time it's for keeps.'

'No,' screamed Blaize, 'I resign. I'm tired of working for some low-life beer-swilling pot-bellied Aussie who wouldn't know a principle if he fell over one.'

Someone in the newsroom sniggered, and Barney was about to round on them when a sudden silence fell. Blaize, unheeding, turned on her heel and walked straight into Cal.

He put out a hand to steady her, his eyes taking in her flushed face and feverish eyes. He looked around at the newsroom. 'What exactly is going on?' His words cracked around the room and everyone stilled.

Barney looked him straight in the eye. 'What's it to you, Mr Smith?'

'A great deal,' said Cal calmly. 'I own the company that has just bought this newspaper. I came in to have a look around and I find World War Three breaking out. I repeat, what is going on?'

The paper's managing director, Andrew Brown, was at Cal's side. 'Things do get a bit noisy in here at times, Mr Smith,' he said uneasily. 'It's all part of the creative process.' He laughed uncertainly and then stopped when he realised that no one else was about to join in. He glanced at Blaize. 'This is Blaize O'Halloran, Mr Smith.'

'We've met,' said Cal briefly.

'Blaize?' said Andrew tentatively. 'Perhaps you can explain?'

'Certainly,' said Blaize. 'Barney and I were having a row over whether I'd just resigned or been sacked. Either way, I'm going and wild horses wouldn't drag me back.'

She looked at Cal and added, 'You'll have to employ a new vulture now.'

'So you're the famous Barney,' remarked Cal, gazing with a half-smile at her erstwhile boss.

'I'm Barney,' replied the news editor. 'I don't know about famous.'

'Allow me to congratulate you on your divorce from

Blaize,' said Cal with a glint in his eye. 'Or should I say Meg Bryan?'

Blaize stood rooted to the spot as she watched Barney being so deftly ridiculed. He looked distinctly uncomfortable. 'Ah, well, Mr Smith, that was all in the nature of the job,' he said uncertainly. 'I'm sure Blaize just picked my name at random to provide her cover. I hope she didn't get in your way too much.'

'Not at all,' smiled Cal, adding blandly, 'although I'm not at all certain about her methods of getting a story. They're certainly original.'

'Great reporter, Blaize. Real talent,' offered Barney.

'You liar,' exploded Blaize. 'That's not what you were saying five minutes ago.'

Barney flashed her one of his rare grins. 'On mature reflection, I've changed my mind. You can have your job back any time you like, Blaize. The team wouldn't be the same without you.'

She glared at Barney and then glanced at Cal. 'I could kill you right now,' she hissed, before turning on her heel and making for her desk.

She ripped open her drawers and began emptying them into a cardboard box. She could feel Cal's eyes on her the whole time, but she could not look up. Bought the newspaper, indeed. So the rumours were true. What was he going to do with it? He didn't know the first thing about newspapers.

Slowly the office regained its normal high level of noise and she glanced up to see Barney deep in conversation with Cal and Andrew. All three men were smiling. Probably some dirty joke. She snorted furiously and rammed some papers into her bag. Men!

'Do you want some help with that?' Without waiting

for an answer Cal picked up her briefcase and rested it on her desk, looking at her.

'No, I do not,' she snapped. 'The last thing I want is help from you. How dare you buy this newspaper?'

'It was for sale,' said Cal calmly.

'You know what I mean,' retorted Blaize furiously. 'I suppose you think you've bought me too now.' She shovelled some heavy books on top of a delicate fern that had stood on her desk. 'Getting Barney to give me my job back like that,' she raged. 'What's everyone supposed to think now?'

'I don't give a stuff what anyone thinks,' replied Cal. 'But I know how much you care about working here.'

'Well, I do,' she said fiercely, 'but you're so patronising it's unbelievable.

'In any case, if I hadn't wanted to get fired I would have said so,' she added illogically. The blood was pounding in her ears now and she felt totally drained after the row with Barney. Being so close to Cal wasn't doing anything for her composure.

'What's the matter?' she snapped, suddenly very close to tears.

Cal lifted an eyebrow. 'What do you mean, "What's the matter?"'

'I mean,' said Blaize wildly, 'have I got spinach on my teeth or a button undone or something?'

'Should you have?' asked Cal. Goddamn him, there was that glint in his eye. He was laughing at her again.

'I only ask,' she retorted, trying to assume a calmness she didn't feel, 'because of the way you were staring at me. Didn't your mother ever tell you it was rude to stare?'

He smiled slightly. 'No,' he said, adding cryptically, 'But she always insisted I should look before I leap.'

'Well, you're not going to leap on me,' Blaize grated.

'Not here, no,' agreed Cal. 'Far too public. No room under your desk and far too much clutter on top of it. Are you always this untidy?' He picked up the scattered print-out of her profile of him and glanced at the first paragraph.

'How very interesting,' he drawled.

'Give that to me,' she yelled.

'You forget,' he said softly, 'I own this newspaper now, right down to the last paper clip. This should provide very interesting reading.' He folded it into his jacket pocket, his eyes on her the whole time. The blush rose in her cheeks until she could feel even the back of her neck was turning pink.

'Stop staring at me,' she muttered.

He shrugged. 'Can't help it, I'm afraid.'

'I'll get you a photograph,' she snapped.

'Oh, I think I can do better than that,' he said softly.

She shrugged, trying hard to cover up her inner turmoil. 'Yes, well, you'll have Sophie's photograph to look at tomorrow.'

He raised his eyebrows questioningly. She swallowed and added, unable to contain her hurt, 'All two point five million of them in glorious colour on page five. Is it true she's going to marry you after the trial?'

Cal had gone very still. 'Blaize——'

But there was no stopping her. 'We need exclusive quotes, you know. And now you own the paper you can probably make the story page one news, instead of just a picture caption on five.'

Cal's jaw muscle tightened. 'Is this true?' he grated.

'Well, you should know,' replied Blaize. 'You're the man who's just bought the paper. I'd get your quotes ready for the evening news if I were you.'

'You know what I mean,' said Cal. 'This stuff about Sophie and me. Is there a story about it?'

'You're the boss man now, Cal,' retorted Blaize. 'Why don't you ask your new employees?'

He looked around at Barney and Andrew, his lips tightening. 'Maybe I will.'

He turned back to her. 'Go down to the front of the building and get in my Rolls,' he ordered. 'I shall join you shortly.'

'No. I'm getting the Tube,' said Blaize doggedly. 'I don't want any more to do with you.'

He gripped her elbow and gave her a little shake. 'For once in your life, Blaize, do as you're bloody well told. You're not well and I'm taking you back to your flat. You're not going on the Tube, by taxi or on a bus. You will go downstairs and you will get in that car if I have to carry you.'

'Just try!' she cried. 'I'll sue you for sexual harassment, constructive dismissal and——'

'Yes—and?' he said, his eyes glinting dangerously.

'And parking on a double yellow line!' she yelled. 'No one's allowed to stop outside the office. I got towed away last week. And I don't see why you shouldn't get the same treatment, Mr Big Shot Smith.'

Cal reached for a file he was holding under his arm. Blaize saw with a sinking feeling that it had her name on it. 'According to this,' he said smoothly, 'you owe the company several hundred pounds in unpaid parking fines, which the firm has so far paid. Also there is a little matter of a hire car which you inexplicably left in a snowdrift in Oxfordshire, and then got a breakdown truck to tow away.'

Blaize fought hard to control her voice. 'You know perfectly well that the front axle was broken. I was told by a so-called expert that I couldn't drive it.'

Cal's expression did not alter by one millimetre. 'According to the garage there was absolutely nothing wrong with the car. Apart from a small dent and a flooded engine.'

Blaize's jaw dropped as the full meaning of what he had just said went home. 'You scheming. . .' she breathed.

'Yes?' said Cal.

Blaize swallowed. 'You tricked me. You knew all the time the car was OK. You. . .' For the first time in her life, words failed her.

'I can't resist a damsel in distress,' said Cal lightly. 'You're definitely a damsel and you would certainly have been in distress if you'd stayed much longer in that car. But you wouldn't have left it to go with me unless you were persuaded it was completely broken.'

'So you lied to me,' breathed Blaize.

'So I lied,' agreed Cal. 'Terrible of me, wasn't it?'

She thought of all that had happened at Cal's home and said nothing. He looked at her face, watching with amusement the different emotions crossing it like cloud shadows.

'Go downstairs, Blaize, and get in my car,' he repeated at last. 'I'm not going to tell you again. We've got a lot of things to talk about. And don't think about giving me the slip. You'll have to confront your emotions and feelings at some stage and I want to be there when you do. There's no point in running away all your life.'

Blaize stared at him defiantly but after a few seconds dropped her eyes. There was no way she could stare him down. But there was no way she was going to get into his car. That was for certain.

She shouldered her bag, hefted the box, and made for the lift. Her legs felt like lead. Cal's chauffeur was sitting in the foyer reading a paper but he sprang up as soon as Blaize stepped out of the lift. 'Hello, miss,' he smiled. 'Let's just relieve you of all this stuff, shall we?'

And before Blaize could say anything he had loaded her bags into the boot of the Rolls and was holding the door open for her. Suddenly it seemed too much trouble to protest any more. She got in the car and sank into the soft leather.

Cal arrived five minutes later. 'Well, that was quite fun,' he said, clambering in beside her.

'Fun?' she repeated. 'The only fun I could think of having there would be skewering Barney and barbecuing him over a fire of all my expenses claims that he's rejected.'

'You obviously haven't got the trick of treating him correctly,' replied Cal.

'Well, you do own the paper,' said Blaize tartly.

'True,' agreed Cal. 'And besides, I have all that inside information on him.' Blaize stared at him questioningly and he smiled. 'You're not the only person who puts in whopping expenses claims in this office, Blaize. Barney is an absolute master at it. Must come from being your "husband".'

'Why, you. . .' Blaize grabbed a cushion and threw it at him but he gripped her wrist and pushed her back into the seat.

'Oh, no, but I——' she began, but whatever she had been going to say was stopped by his kiss.

At the flat Cal took her keys from her hand and opened the door.

'I never thought I'd say this, considering how much time I spend loathing and despising you,' said Blaize, 'but thanks.'

'You don't loathe and despise me, you love me,' he said, following her in. 'But that's quite all right.'

She stared at him, her heart beating faster at what he had said, but determined to ignore it. 'What exactly do you think you are doing?'

'I spoke to Ned this morning. He and Marie are going away for a few days.'

'I know,' said Blaize. 'What's that got to do with anything?'

Cal sighed exasperatedly. 'It's got to do with the fact that you're not staying here on your own, Blaize. You're not well.'

'I can manage perfectly well, thank you very much,' she said as firmly as she could.

He opened her bedroom door and motioned her inside. 'Get in there and get into bed.'

She leant against the wall. 'I bet you say that to all the girls.'

He reached out and took a strand of her hair. 'Blaize,' he said gently.

'Yes?'

'If you don't stop behaving like a six-year-old I shall put you across my knee and give you a good spanking, flu or no flu.'

She looked into his eyes and swallowed.

'Well?' he challenged.

With a strangled sob she fled into her room and banged the door. She was absolutely certain she could hear him laughing. Rebelliously she tore off her clothes, pulled on an outsize T-shirt and crawled into bed. Suddenly she didn't care about how much she wanted to stamp on Cal's toes. She pulled the duvet over her head and closed her eyes. Heaven.

A shifting in the mattress told her she was not alone. She flicked her eyes open and cautiously burrowed out of the duvet. A pair of amused brown eyes met hers. Cal held out a steaming mug and two aspirins. 'Here. Take this.'

'What is it?' she said cautiously, peering at the amber-coloured liquid.

'Hot toddy. Whisky, hot water and sugar. It'll make you sleep.'

She pulled herself up and grasped the mug. 'I won't get drunk, will I?' she said suspiciously.

'Of course.' He nodded. 'And then while you're sleeping I'll have my evil way with you, before rifling through your jewel box and stealing out of your life for ever.'

She glared at him and downed the contents. 'The last part doesn't sound such a bad idea,' she retorted. But he had been right, the drink was beginning to make her feel wonderfully relaxed and warm. He got up. 'Where are you going?' she asked, more tremulously than she meant to.

He walked back across the room swiftly and, bending down, kissed her on the cheek. 'Just into the next room. I've got a lot of paperwork to catch up on. Mind if I use your telephone?' She shook her head sleepily and fell back on the pillows. If anybody had told her two hours before that Cal Smith would be tucking her up in bed as carefully as a mother hen she would have laughed in their face. Wonders would never cease. Smiling slightly, she fell asleep.

She woke early next morning, feeling wonderfully refreshed. The flu symptoms had almost completely disappeared. She got up and, wandering into the sitting-room, saw through an open door Cal asleep on Ned's bed. She walked into the room and smiled at his sleeping face. It was impossible not to like him when he looked like that. She leant over to push the duvet more securely round him and gasped as he pulled her down beside him. 'I was hoping for a hot water bottle,' he remarked sleepily, 'but you're a much better idea.'

'Thanks,' she said shortly.

'Relax, Blaize,' he whispered. 'What's the matter with you?'

'You know exactly what's the matter with me,' she began.

But Cal interrupted before she could continue. 'Yes,' he said thoughtfully, 'I do. You're too nervy by half. We got off to a bad start, but whereas I've forgiven you, you still think of me in terms of a big bad wolf.'

'You tried to bribe me,' she said. 'And——'

'Yes?' he prompted.

'You said you didn't like me,' she muttered. 'Oh, God, that sounds so pathetic, but I felt really attracted to you, even when I thought you were just a big crook, and I thought you felt the same about me. But when you said you didn't like me and then we made love I felt—I felt——' She stopped suddenly. She couldn't go on. It was like letting him into her heart and she'd never allowed anyone to get that close to her before.

'What did you feel?' he persisted gently.

'I felt you were just using me,' she blurted out. 'But in a stupid way I was even content with that because you were close to me. And then I thought you were going to give me the brush-off and I couldn't bear it. That's why I made up that silly story about Ned being my fiancé.'

She gulped and then added, 'That night in the restaurant I thought everything was going to sort itself out, but when you confirmed it had all been a meaningless fling as far as you were concerned, and then tried to bribe me, I felt like the lowest of the low.' Tears were running down her face and he pulled her gently towards him.

'Blaize,' he said softly, 'I wasn't going to give you the brush-off the day after we made love, or any other day, but the way you reacted made me feel that perhaps it had meant nothing to you. I guess I wasn't really thinking very clearly. I had a lot on my plate. But I only said that stuff in the restaurant for the benefit of the tape. I didn't want the entire fraud squad to get a ringside seat on our emotions.'

Blaize stared at his face and smiled shakily. 'I can't help myself when I look at you, Cal. You just turn all my emotions completely upside-down. I've never felt about anyone the way I feel about you.'

He bent to kiss her throat and his hands moved up her body, his fingers fluttering against her stomach and breasts. 'God, I've missed you,' he muttered.

His hands stilled and he pulled her closer to him. 'We started this whole thing on completely the wrong foot,' he said. 'But we can start again on the right one now. We've got a whole lifetime's worth of talking to do.'

'Is that an interview?' muttered Blaize.

'Mmm,' he replied, kissing the tip of her nose. 'Exclusive.'

Blaize gasped as his fingers stripped off her T-shirt and then trailed over her skin, inviting a shuddering response that came straight from her soul. His hands were stroking her breasts, his lips caressing their warm rose-tipped curves.

She sighed and twisted in his arms, arching her body to him in mute appeal, wanting him even more fiercely than she had wanted him before, needing to surrender totally to a love she could no longer deny.

Her hands clasped around his long, lean body,

pulling him to her, demanding that he take control of the fire leaping through her veins.

And then he had pushed her back on the bed, stroking her body with the concentrated desire that Sean had never shown. His lips travelled over her warm nakedness and she felt the rhythm of passion Cal had awoken in her move her body against his.

'Easy, Blaize, easy,' he whispered. 'We've got all the time in the world.' But time and space had shrunk to the distance of their gaze and Blaize was no longer mistress of her feelings.

She was unable to control the deep shuddering gasps that he was drawing from her very soul. 'Please, Cal, please,' she cried in an appeal that she was hardly aware of, and then, almost as if she had been tipped over a rollercoaster, pleasure overtook every conscious fibre in her mind. One tiny, almost soundless gasp came from her throat and then her feelings floated free as she felt Cal's body shake in her arms.

In the aftermath she felt a peace she had never before realised existed. Cal pulled her head down on to his chest and within minutes she was fast asleep.

It was about two hours later, Blaize supposed, when she awoke. Cal was not beside her but there was still a core of warmth in the rumpled sheets next to her to show where he had been. Happily she wriggled into it, soaking up the comfort of being where he had lain.

For a while she dozed and then, beginning to wonder what had happened to him, got out of bed and, pulling her T-shirt back on, padded into the living-room. Cal was not there, but there was a note left for her on the kitchen table.

'Darling Blaize,' she read, 'Sophie called me, she needs me badly. Will call you later. Love, Cal.'

Blaize sat down with a bump, suddenly overwhelmed with unspeakable bitterness as she realised that Cal had left her bed to go to another woman.

How could he have done this to her? Did her feelings mean nothing? Sophie Harrison and Cal. It was going to be like Sean all over again. Blaize clenched her jaw as she thought of the last few hours. She remembered their lovemaking as if she had been watching from the ceiling and swallowed, with a sick feeling in the pit of her stomach. God, how easy it must have been for him.

She stood up suddenly. He had made a fool of her twice. He was not going to get a third chance. She never wanted to see Cal Smith again.

CHAPTER TEN

THE telephone rang so shrilly in the silence that Blaize almost leapt into the air.

'Please, God,' she muttered as she lifted the receiver with trembling fingers. 'Please don't let it be Cal.' For all her anger she knew that one word from him could stifle her resolve to make a clean break. A man like Cal, as she knew to her cost, was almost impossible to withstand.

But it was Cal. His voice sounded hurried, without its usual calm assurance. Perhaps even he, with all his arrogance, had realised the folly of leaving such an explicit message for her. 'Blaize, did you get my note?'

'I got it,' she said grimly.

'I'm still at Sophie's,' he said.

'How tiresome for you,' Blaize muttered.

The static on his cell phone line was fairly bad and the tension in her voice was lost on him.

'Look,' he explained, 'I've come out to the car to make the call because I can't really be speaking to you like this from the house.'

Blaize's heart chilled at his words. She suddenly realised she was gripping the receiver so tightly her fingers hurt. It was surprising really that it didn't snap in two.

'Blaize?'

'Still here,' she replied dully.

'I'm sorry, love, but I haven't got time to explain what's going on at the moment. I just thought I'd ring to make sure you were OK.'

'Very considerate of you, I'm sure,' muttered Blaize. 'And how is Sophie?' she added acidly.

'Sophie?' repeated Cal, sounding momentarily taken aback. 'She's bearing up very well, all things considered.'

'How nice,' said Blaize, trying to keep control of her rapidly growing temper. What did he mean, Sophie was very well, all things considered? Perhaps he'd decided to confess to Sophie about whose bed he'd just left. Well, how wonderfully understanding of her.

'Blaize?'

'Still here,' she snapped again, resisting the temptation to add, 'But not for long.' There was no use in telling him anything now. She would choke if she had to speak to him for much longer.

'Blaize, look, I can't stay long, but is there something wrong? You sound upset.'

She sucked in her breath. He sounded so genuinely concerned too, blast him. No wonder she had been taken in by him. 'Nothing,' she muttered. 'I have to go now.' And blindly, before the tears started to course down her cheeks, she hung up.

She dressed mechanically and, pulling on a coat, made for the door. Maybe a walk in the park would clear her brain, help her decide what to do next. If Cal had any sensitivity at all he wouldn't come back. But sensitivity was obviously what he most lacked, otherwise he would never have subjected her to such a phone call.

She thought of the note he had left and sighed. Word for word it was almost exactly the same as the one she had heard on the telephone answering machine. It was obvious that when Sophie wanted him he would always go to her, no matter what.

But she, Blaize, didn't have to put up with the

situation. Indeed, she thought with a particularly violent kick at some snow in the park, she would not put up with it. Cal Smith might have an ego the size of an elephant and a hide to match, but there was no way she had to pander to him.

She finally made her way home, weary and chilled to the bone, and her heart rose into her mouth when the lift opened on to her floor and she made out his dark bulk waiting against the door of the flat.

She stared up at his frame as he barred the way inside and swallowed. 'Let me by, please,' she said with a calm bravery she did not feel.

But he stood his ground, putting a hand under her elbow. 'Look, Blaize, I realise what you're thinking. I realised as soon as you put the phone down that you had jumped to some stupid conclusion about Sophie and me.'

Blaize said nothing. She did not dare even try in case she burst into tears. He shook her elbow gently. 'I know how it must appear to you, but really we have to talk.'

It was the gentleness of his tone that finally battered down her icy façade. 'How the hell do you know what I think, you two-timing rat?' yelled Blaize.

Cal's face darkened. 'Go on,' she continued, lifting her chin into the air. 'Get out of my life. Now.'

He took her by both arms and shook her. 'Don't you know how I feel about you?' he said fiercely. 'I swear I wouldn't lay a finger on you, but sometimes, I have to admit, I want to shake you until your teeth rattle. You continually see me in a bad light.'

'I don't want to see you at all,' she cried. 'Not any more, Cal Smith. I know a complete swine when I see one. Get the hell out of my way and get the hell out of my life.'

'You'll see me and you'll listen to me, Blaize,' he grated, 'even if I have to camp outside your flat. You've taken the contents of a hastily written note and twisted their meaning into something quite fantastic.'

'I would have thought the meaning was perfectly plain,' said Blaize, 'but I wouldn't bother standing here and spinning me some tale when Sophie Harrison's waiting. I mean, I quite understand. Gentlemen prefer blondes, so I've been told. But I shouldn't look too closely at her roots if I were you.'

'You're being completely over the top,' retorted Cal. 'Plus you don't know what you're talking about.'

'Good,' yelled Blaize. 'I don't want to be an expert on deceit.' She shook her arm from his grip and backed away from him, her eyes glittering with unshed tears, before she turned and ran down the stairs.

'Blaize!' he shouted. She could hear the thump on the steps as he began to run after her. She felt like a hunted animal, her heart pounding in her chest, a tight pain in her lungs as she strove to run ever faster. She had to get away. Had to.

Outside she gained valuable seconds on him when she dodged around a corner.

Her own car had been parked outside for several days, ever since she had picked up the hire car to go to Oxfordshire, but it fired first go. Cal was only a few feet behind her now, his hand reaching for the door-handle, but she put her foot flat on the floor and scorched up the road as if driving for her life. One look in her rear-view mirror showed him standing in the middle of the road, staring starkly after her.

Blaize looked at her rucksack and went over her mental list again. Money, passport, camera—if she had forgotten anything now it was just too bad.

'You don't have to go,' said Ned. 'It's only ten days
until Christmas and you'll be all alone on the other
side of the world.'

'I don't care,' said Blaize. 'If I'm going to be
miserable I might as well go the whole hog.'

Ned sighed. 'You're being ridiculous, Blaize, and
you know it. Can't you just tell me what's going on?
Why don't you and Cal at least talk? I mean,' he
added placatingly, 'there could be some really simple
explanation for his behaviour.'

'We have nothing to talk about,' replied Blaize,
shortly.

'I'm sure he's got someone watching the flat,' mused
Ned. 'I can't tell whether it's because he wants to
know where you've gone or whether he suspects you
of having some other lover.'

'He's got a nerve,' said Blaize hotly. 'He's the expert
two-timer. It's just like Sean all over again. Why I
have to fall for men like that I'll never know, but I
don't have to continue to make a fool of myself.'

Ned sighed. 'I'm sure you're wrong, Blaize. Why
don't you give him a chance? For all his reputation, he
really is a nice guy.'

'He's a cheat and a liar and I never want to see him
again,' said Blaize flatly.

Ned shrugged. 'I wouldn't put it past him to follow
you all the way to South America once he finds out
where you're going.'

'I hope he crashes in the Matto Grosso,' retorted
Blaize. 'There is absolutely nothing he could say to me
that would make me think well of him.'

'He thinks pretty highly of you,' said Ned.

Blaize said nothing. She had spent the last few days
at Marie's flat. The two girls had instantly hit it off
when Ned introduced them, and it had been the

sparkly good-natured French girl who suggested Blaize
stay with her until her emotions had cooled a little.

'Absence as well as absinthe makes the heart grow
fonder,' she joked, 'and if this Cal really feels for you
then he will respect your hurt feelings.'

Blaize had been there a week now, but she had not
been idle. She had sent in her resignation letter to the
newspaper and spent most of her savings on a ticket to
Peru. She had picked her destination at random. It
sounded nice and far away.

'There's a civil war going on there at the moment,'
warned Ned.

'Good,' said Blaize. 'I could do with a nice peaceful
civil war. It will be very restful in comparison with
everything that's happened to me in the last few
weeks.'

'Blaize, don't do this,' pleaded Ned. 'Marie and I
will worry ourselves sick over you.'

'I'll be all right,' soothed Blaize. 'I've got to get
away, Ned. I just can't stay here any more. Maybe I'll
come back quite soon. I just want to get Cal out of my
system.'

'You'll never do that,' said Ned.

Blaize looked at him sharply. 'What do you mean?'

'Look, sis, I saw the way you looked at each other
that day I came to pick you up at his house in
Oxfordshire. Even though you were furious with each
other, your body language was just so obvious. He was
so jealous of me when you said I was your fiancé I
really thought he was going to go for me.'

'Don't be silly,' said Blaize, attempting a lightness
she did not feel. 'Cal thinks about women in much the
same way as I do about chocolate biscuits. He has one
and then another and another and pretty soon the
whole packet's finished. And Sophie's just another one

in the pile. Well, maybe she can put up with his two-timing, but I can't. She can have him and good riddance.'

'You're wrong about him,' said Ned stubbornly. 'He doesn't think that way about you.'

'Oh, go away and leave me in peace!' yelled Blaize, her patience finally snapping.

Ned lifted his hands helplessly. 'OK, I'm going. I'm going.'

Blaize saw him out of the flat and then lay down on the sofa with a book. But she didn't read it. The vision of Cal's face kept looming in front of her. Damn him.

The doorbell rang and she swore under her breath. Who was it this time? She was unable to believe her eyes when she opened the door. Sophie Harrison was standing on the threshold. The blonde smiled nervously at Blaize. 'May I come in?'

Speechless, Blaize stood aside and motioned the elegant woman into the sitting-room. Sophie stood in the centre of the room like a deer who knew it was being tracked by a tiger.

Blaize leant against the door-jamb and folded her arms. 'Well? I won't ask you to sit down, I can't imagine that you will be staying very long.'

Sophie put her handbag on the table and turned to meet Blaize's accusing stare. 'I've come here to explain a few things to you, Blaize. Don't make it more difficult for me than it already is.'

'My heart bleeds for you,' said Blaize bitterly. 'How did you find me? Hire a team of snoopers?'

'Your brother told me.'

Blaize's jaw dropped. 'He did what?' she said weakly.

'You heard,' said Sophie grimly. 'You're so intent on nursing your wounded pride that you don't give one second's thought to the fact that you could be wrong about Cal. That you *are* wrong about Cal.'

'So he sends you to plead his case for him,' snapped Blaize. 'I thought it was impossible for him to zoom any further down in my estimation. I was wrong.'

Sophie shook her head. 'Cal didn't send me here. He doesn't know anything about my visit. He'd blow a gasket if he knew what I was doing.'

'So what are you doing?'

'Listen, Blaize,' said Sophie exasperatedly, 'I am trying to help you. I owe Cal a lot and by coming here I hoped I could pay back some of that debt.'

'What's he done for you that he hasn't done with me?' snarled Blaize.

'He hasn't slept with me, for a start,' spat Sophie. 'I am trying to tell you that Cal and I have never been romantically linked, except in the over-heated imagination of some newspaper reporters.'

Blaize stared at her in astonishment. The withering put-down that she had been going to make died on her lips. 'I don't believe you,' she said coldly.

'Don't you ever read a newspaper?' demanded Sophie.

Blaize shrugged. 'I haven't seen one for more than a week. I don't work for newspapers any more. And I haven't watched the TV much either, except for the odd film.'

The other woman sighed and reached in her bag. 'Then you'd better read this,' she said, handing over a newspaper several days old.

Blaize smoothed out the creased paper and gasped at the headline. The large print screamed out 'Life Saver!' and below was a smaller heading: 'Smith Talks Fraud Case Director out of Suicide Bid'. There were pictures of Cal and Sophie's husband, the man she had seen plead not guilty to the fraud only a few days before.

'It's quite simple,' said Sophie. 'The story is about Cal saving John's life.' Her voice trembled slightly but she steadied it and went on bravely. 'My husband has been under tremendous stress during the last few months. You can't begin to understand the pressures he's been through. I don't think anyone can, really. He started behaving irrationally, had violent tempers, and then black depression. And the only one who can talk him out of it is Cal. When John gets really black I ring up Cal and ask him to come round. Sometimes the situation at home is quite desperate.'

Blaize thought of the words Sophie had used on the answering machine and winced at all the wrong conclusions to which she had jumped.

'Then, when John was charged, he seemed to become completely unbalanced. But Cal could always calm him. It's because he's such a good listener, I suppose.'

Blaize nodded. Sophie didn't need to tell her how good a listener Cal was. The older woman sighed and continued. 'Then John got a gun from somewhere, God knows where, and he absolutely petrified me. He was completely terrifying, you know,' she said, staring calmly at Blaize. 'He didn't even look like the man I loved and married, and he was threatening to go out and shoot his fellow directors.

'The only thing that seemed to calm him was the idea of seeing Cal, so I rang his office and they gave me your number. Cal put himself at quite a bit of risk, you know,' added Sophie. 'I thought for one moment he might even get shot, but he disarmed John, and you can't know how grateful I am to him for his support and kindness.

'I'm sorry, Blaize, that it all ended in such a stupid misunderstanding—that's why I've come here today. But I had to ring. You must see that.'

'Yes,' said Blaize numbly, 'I do see. But I don't understand why he didn't tell me.'

'You didn't actually give him a chance,' said Sophie gently. 'He came as soon as I called, and he told me he'd left you a note. Didn't you get it?'

Blaize sat down on the sofa with a bump. 'Yes, I got it,' she muttered.

Sophie sat down beside her. 'What I don't understand is what Cal must have said to you when he slipped out of the house to ring you up from his car. He's normally so clear in what he says, but somehow you must have got hold of the wrong end of the stick.' She grasped Blaize's hand. 'Am I right?'

Blaize looked up at the older woman's compassionate face. 'Yes,' she admitted. 'Quite right.' She smiled and shrugged her shoulders. 'I've been so stupid, Sophie, so damn stupid.'

'We all are occasionally,' said Sophie with an understanding smile.

Blaize smiled back. 'How's your husband?' she asked.

'He'll pull through,' said Sophie, standing up. 'He's completely innocent of any fraud, you know. I'm going to help him fight this all the way—but not,' she added definitely, 'with a gun.

'Cal's offered to supply the best barrister he can get. He feels it's partly his fault that John's facing charges, but I know my husband used to sign papers without even looking at them. He was just so tired all the time.'

Sophie shut her handbag with a snap and turned back to Blaize. 'Cal thinks a great deal of you, you

know. He talks about you all the time. I've never seen
him so upset as he has been in the last few days.'

'Upset?' repeated Blaize, startled. She had never
imagined Cal being upset over anything.

'Oh, he doesn't go about tearing his hair and beating
his chest in despair,' said Sophie with a small smile.
'He's not the type. But he's been having some blinding
rages recently. His secretary was considering giving
her notice. I know he finally snapped with that useless
gardener of his at his home in Oxfordshire. Something
about leaving a rotten ladder lying around. Anyway,
he's now without a cook or a gardener and existing, so
I gather, on baked beans and something rather revolt-
ing called egg surprise.'

Blaize got up hurriedly. The picture of Cal in the
manor house kitchen was so vivid she felt as though all
the air had been let out of her lungs.

'Thank you for coming, Sophie. I'm sorry I was so
rotten to you.'

The older woman gripped her hand. 'Don't even
think about it. If you love Cal as much as I love John,
then I can understand why you felt so jealous about
him. It's just silly to let that ruin your happiness when
there's no cause.'

At the front door, Sophie paused and turned. 'This
may be awfully presumptuous of me, but if you want
to see Cal he's at his house in Oxfordshire today,
interviewing potential new cooks.'

Blaize grinned at her. 'Thanks, Sophie. Thanks a
lot. You can be presumptuous any time you like.'

She closed the door behind her unexpected visitor
and stood for a moment regarding the flat, then, her
mind made up, she grabbed her handbag, slammed
the door behind her and ran down to the street to her
car. Within seconds she was gunning it down the street.

'Come on, come on,' she muttered, her foot flat on the accelerator as she weaved in and out of the traffic and on to the M40. Whatever the record was for getting from London to Oxfordshire, she was going to break it.

Once again in the snowy country lanes, she slowed down. There was no way she was going to have an accident like the last time. Halfway there she remembered she had never actually driven to Cal's house before, but vague memories of landmarks they had passed when Ned had come to pick them up helped her find her way.

She seemed possessed by some sheer animal instinct that never let her take a wrong turn. Within a very short time she was shooting through the manor gates, the icy gravel spitting from her tyres.

She slowed as she neared the house and began to consider the problem of getting into the house and, more difficult, what exactly she was going to say to Cal when she saw him.

There were six cars parked in front of the house. They must belong to the prospective cooks. Blaize smiled and drove around the back, parking in the stable block. Then, taking her courage in both hands, she walked quickly up to the kitchen door, her heart pounding at what she had decided to do.

The door was open and there was no one in the kitchen. No one except Conor, who heaved joyfully to his feet and practically knocked her over with his welcome. Thankfully he didn't bark.

'Come on, Conor,' she whispered. 'Let's see off the opposition.'

The six women sitting in Cal's sitting-room looked up as Blaize entered. She coughed discreetly and they all eyed her expectantly.

She smiled around with brief professional courtesy. 'I'm sorry, ladies,' she announced, 'but Mr Smith has been called away unexpectedly. He will of course pay your travelling expenses and we will contact you soon with another suitable date.'

One of the women looked haughtily at Blaize's jeans and sweatshirt. 'And who are you? I didn't see you on the way in.'

'No,' smiled Blaize, side-stepping her question. 'I was out the back feeding Conor.' She stood aside as the enormous wolfhound padded amiably into the room. As one woman the prospective cooks got to their feet and fled.

Blaize flattened herself against the sitting-room door and grinned broadly at their retreating backs. Her first objective had proved a complete push-over. But she was not so certain about the next.

Her heart almost in her mouth, Blaize tapped on Cal's study door. 'Go away,' he shouted. 'I'm in the middle of an important phone call.'

Blaize opened the door and walked in. 'I'm sorry,' she said, 'but this won't wait.'

Cal stopped in the middle of a sentence to a New York banker and dropped the receiver back into its cradle. 'Blaize!' he said, astonished.

She walked up to the desk. 'I'm sorry, Cal. I found out about John Harrison this morning and what you did. I was suspicious, narrow-minded and behaved in a completely over-the-top fashion.'

He stared at her for a long moment. 'Anything else?' he said at last.

She bit her lip and raised her eyes to his. 'There is just one more, very small thing.'

He looked at her questioningly and she could feel herself blushing under his gaze, but having come this

far she was not going to chicken out now. She lifted
her chin and stared right back at him 'I love you,
Cal.'

He sat back in his chair and stared at her.

She swallowed, determined not to let the silence
press in on them any longer, and added in a small
voice, 'I suppose I could just say happy Christmas and
get out of your life.'

He grinned and opened his arms. 'Come here,' he
said softly. 'Right now.'

A small fire burned in the bedroom grate and Blaize
stared dreamily at the flames. Conor shifted his huge
bulk by the door and grunted happily to himself.

'It's no good,' said Cal. 'That dog is ruined. I can't
imagine him putting up with sleeping in the stables
ever again.'

'Strange,' replied Blaize, 'when you consider how
cosy and warm it was in there.'

Cal smiled and pulled her warm body closer to his.
'On the whole, I think I prefer to have real home
comforts.'

The memory of their lovemaking was like a warm
imprint on her body. Cal had carried her upstairs
before the last of the cooks had properly disappeared
through the manor gates.

It was as though the two of them had an all-
consuming shared hunger that recognised their deep
need for each other, that could never be quenched.
And now, overwhelmed by a dreamy languor, Blaize
sighed and traced a pattern on Cal's bare chest, trying
at the same time to get even closer, if that was possible,
to him.

'Of course,' she murmured, 'I could have been in
Peru now.'

'Unlikely,' he replied. 'There was no way I would have allowed you to get on that plane.'

'I don't see how you could have stopped me,' she said, smiling at his calm arrogance.

'Quite simple really, sweetheart. I'd arranged to have you arrested.'

She sat up suddenly and stared at him. 'You what?'

'You heard.' His hand enclosed her fingers and he smiled at her. 'I wasn't going to let my future wife risk her neck on the other side of the world. Ned agreed, as a matter of fact. So he was going to detain you until the plane went.'

Blaize's mouth fell open. 'I'd have sued you for wrongful arrest.'

'Yes,' he said simply. 'But you'd have had to stay in the country to do that, so I would still have achieved my objective.'

'Do you always go about getting things in such a single-minded way?' she enquired.

'Only things I really want,' he said reflectively. 'Although it was me who nearly messed the whole thing up. I should have told you properly about John Harrison when I rang from my car that morning. But I just felt I didn't have time. I never even considered you would think I was having an affair with Sophie. I was just so focused on you.'

'Well, it wasn't all your fault,' said Blaize. 'I just didn't listen to you when you kept saying you wanted to talk to me. I thought it was just going to be. . .' She faltered, unable to say how she had really felt.

'What?' prompted Cal.

Blaize shrugged and then opened up. 'I don't know really. I was too scared to talk about feelings. I didn't want to let you into my heart.'

Cal's hand caressed her breast and he leant to kiss her. 'And now?' he questioned.

'Now?' she murmured. 'Now you've got exclusive rights to it.'

Look out for Temptation's bright, new, stylish covers...

They're Terrifically Tempting!

We're sure you'll love the new raspberry-coloured Temptation books—our brand new look from December.

Temptation romances are still as passionate and fun-loving as ever and they're on sale now!

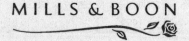

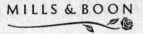

Cruel Legacy

One man's untimely death deprives a wife of her husband, robs a man of his job and offers someone else the chance of a lifetime...

Suicide — the only way out for Andrew Ryecart, facing crippling debt. An end to his troubles, but for those he leaves behind the problems are just beginning, as the repercussions of this most desperate of acts reach out and touch the lives of six different people — changing them forever.

Special large-format paperback edition

**OCTOBER
£8.99**

WORLDWIDE

Next Month's Romances

Each month you can choose from a wide variety of romance with Mills & Boon. Below are the new titles to look out for next month, why not ask either Mills & Boon Reader Service or your Newsagent to reserve you a copy of the titles you want to buy – just tick the titles you would like and either post to Reader Service or take it to any Newsagent and ask them to order your books.

Please save me the following titles: Please tick

		✓
TRIAL BY MARRIAGE	*Lindsay Armstrong*	
ONE FATEFUL SUMMER	*Margaret Way*	
WAR OF LOVE	*Carole Mortimer*	
A SECRET INFATUATION	*Betty Neels*	
ANGELS DO HAVE WINGS	*Helen Brooks*	
MOONSHADOW MAN	*Jessica Hart*	
SWEET DESIRE	*Rosemary Badger*	
NO TIES	*Rosemary Gibson*	
A PHYSICAL AFFAIR	*Lynsey Stevens*	
TRIAL IN THE SUN	*Kay Thorpe*	
IT STARTED WITH A KISS	*Mary Lyons*	
A BURNING PASSION	*Cathy Williams*	
GAMES LOVERS PLAY	*Rosemary Carter*	
HOT NOVEMBER	*Ann Charlton*	
DANGEROUS DISCOVERY	*Laura Martin*	
THE UNEXPECTED LANDLORD	*Leigh Michaels*	

If you would like to order these books in addition to your regular subscription from Mills & Boon Reader Service please send £1.90 per title to: Mills & Boon Reader Service, Freepost, P.O. Box 236, Croydon, Surrey, CR9 9EL, quote your Subscriber No:.................................. (if applicable) and complete the name and address details below. Alternatively, these books are available from many local Newsagents including W H Smith, J Menzies, Martins and other paperback stockists from 13 January 1995.

Name:..

Address:..

..............................Post Code:........................

To Retailer: If you would like to stock M&B books please contact your regular book/magazine wholesaler for details.

You may be mailed with offers from other reputable companies as a result of this application. If you would rather not take advantage of these opportunities please tick box.   ☐